PLEASE STAY AWHILE

For the last four years, since her father's death, Fliss Crosby has helped her mother run their small hotel on the Cornish coast. After a poor summer season, they decide to offer winter lets at reduced rates, and Matt Forbes, a handsome writer, comes to stay as a long-term guest. Fliss finds herself becoming increasingly attracted to Matt, but he is strangely secretive about his life. Her doubts about him begin to grow — especially when things start to go wrong in the hotel.

CHRISSIE LOVEDAY

PLEASE STAY AWHILE

Complete and Unabridged

LINFORD
Leicester

First published in Great Britain in 2002

First Linford Edition
published 2003

British Library CIP Data

Loveday, Chrissie
    Please stay awhile.—Large print ed.—
Linford romance library
    1. Love stories
    2. Large type books
    I. Title
    823.9′14 [F]

    ISBN 0–7089–4908–8

Published by
F. A. Thorpe (Publishing)
Anstey, Leicestershire

Set by Words & Graphics Ltd.
Anstey, Leicestershire
Printed and bound in Great Britain by
T. J. International Ltd., Padstow, Cornwall

This book is printed on acid-free paper

1

But we've got to do something, Mum, or we might as well put up the FOR SALE boards right now,' Fliss Crosby pleaded anxiously.

'Well, I wish you'd tell me exactly what we can do. I'm sick to the back teeth with the worry of it all. If only I'd known . . . '

'Yes, Mum, I know.'

Fliss took a deep breath which mixed itself with a sigh and a gulp at the same time and made her choke.

'See? It's starting to affect you, too.'

'What is?' she spluttered.

'The worry of it all. Perhaps we should simply sell up and go and live somewhere exotic.'

'Penmore is about as exotic as it gets in our financial circles. We'd get nothing like the real value for this place. Everybody wants a bargain.'

Fliss and her mother talked late into the night. It was October and the end of the holiday season for another year. Their small hotel on the Cornish coast had more or less finished with visitors for the year and there were no more firm bookings until the Christmas period. It had been a poor season and the anticipated bills were barely covered by the takings. But part with the hotel? Never, Fliss thought. The old building was redolent with memories of smugglers, pirates and even claimed the odd ghost or two. None of it bothered her, as she'd grown up knowing and loving the whole place.

Since Dad had died four years ago, they'd struggled to keep things going, with the help of casual labour. Now, it was serious crunch time. By the following morning, decisions had been made. They would advertise winter lets for a reduced rate. They would also sign on with various agencies. Her mother had been getting quite carried away with that idea ever since she had seen some TV drama with a hotel full of long stay, eccentric guests. Perhaps, most radical of all, Fliss was going to get a job. She had excellent word processing skills and had known every inch of the hotel business since childhood. It couldn't be so difficult to find something here in Cornwall.

Come November, Mrs Crosby stood smiling behind the reception desk. The scheme looked as if it was going to work. They already had two ladies staying and a number of other enquiries. The first two ladies claimed to be artists but after a week, all they seemed to do was sit in front of the fire and chat comfortably. Not that Mrs Crosby minded. She was delighted to have the time to relax a little.

Now, the third of their long-term guests was due to arrive. Matt Forbes was a writer. It didn't matter what he wrote but having an apparently well-known author staying was most exciting. He had a book to finish and had made a reservation for two months. Fliss had told her mother not to be too excited. Lots of people called themselves writers these days.

He was probably some fuddy-duddy chap who wrote railway books or was an authority on pigeon fancying for beginners. Sally Crosby glanced at her watch. He had said sometime before lunch but it was already almost one o'clock. The phone rang.

'Has he arrived yet?' Fliss asked.

She was at work, having been lucky enough to get a job almost immediately the decision had been made. The local radio station had advertised for someone to stand in while the usual receptionist was taking maternity leave. Fliss's wage was going to be a great help towards saving their home and business. Next year just had to be better.

'Has who arrived?' Sally asked irritatingly.

'Our potential Booker Prizewinner, of course.'

'No, not yet.'

'Hope he's going to turn up. We need him,' Fliss said in a worried voice.

'He's only an hour late. You know how difficult it is to find us. I suspect he's driving round in circles somewhere west of Bodmin.'

'Hope so. Give me a call when he's settled.'

'Right. Oh, dear . . . ' she broke off.

'Mum, what's wrong?' Fliss demanded.

'Nothing. He's here. I think it must be him, and cancel fuddy-duddy. There's some sort of Greek hero-type walking down the path. Oh, Fliss, if this is him, he's gorgeous. Even makes my ancient heart flutter a bit. A Greek god, honestly.'

'Mother! Really,' Fliss exploded. 'Control yourself. And smile at him, for goodness' sake.'

'Yes . . . '

The voice tailed away before the phone was dropped, hopefully back into the cradle.

'Mum?' Fliss called again but the

phone was dead.

Really, her mother was quite hopeless. All the same, this resident did sound enticing. It looked promising. Was he married? Why did he need to cut himself off from civilisation? Her mind was racing. The phone rang again and she picked it up absentmindedly.

'Penmore Point Hotel,' she said.

'What?' the voice snapped on the other end. 'I was trying to get Cornwall Radio.'

'I'm sorry,' Fliss apologised as she came back to earth. 'Sorry, this is Cornwall Radio. My mind was just off target.'

'I'm calling to protest about that man who was trying to promote his business on the programme today. It isn't the sort of thing we listeners want to hear.'

Floss went through her usual routine of pacifying the irate woman, trying hard to dismiss thoughts of the hotel's new arrival from her mind.

For once, she could hardly wait for work to end that day. She had already fallen deeply in love with broadcasting and felt certain it was somewhere here that her future might lie. All the same, a Greek god in one's own home sounded even more attractive. Everything looked as if it was going pretty well. The guests were being offered a much simplified version of their usual services, so that her mother could cope alone with the evening meal. That way, they didn't have to pay for a chef's salary.

And now they had the pleasure of a new male guest who sounded more than a little interesting. It was about time, Fliss sighed. She'd had no man in her life since Mark had gone away to the big city to earn his fortune. Dear old Mark, she thought, hoping he was indeed earning his fortune. They'd grown up together and though they'd gone out together for years, there was never that magic spark between them.

When Fliss arrived home, she saw that the car park contained several vehicles. She looked at them, trying to speculate which belonged to Matt

Forbes. The two artist ladies had a small Fiesta and there were a couple more small cars, probably owned by walkers who'd left their cars to strike out along the coastal path. The large people-carrier type must belong to Matt. Oh, no, she muttered. That must mean he had a family. No-one on their own would drive such a large vehicle.

She parked near to it and glanced into the back as she passed. There was no evidence of family; no child car seats or empty sweet bags or stray toys littering the floor. It was neat, clean and quite new. Whoever owned it was obviously fairly well-off, to be able to afford the large vehicle. She gave a sigh and went inside. She had to face helping her mother with the evening meal and socialising with the two ladies. Hopefully, the Greek god would also appear to lighten the load, though he had become marginally less interesting now she knew he might have family.

'Hi, Mum. I'm back,' she called out as she burst into the kitchen.

'Hello, dear. Had a good day?' her mother asked automatically.

'Not bad. How's everything?'

'Hang on a minute. I've just got to finish piping these profiteroles.'

She squeezed the bag to get out the last of the mixture.

'There. Think that should be enough, don't you?'

'Have we got an extra two dozen guests?' Fliss demanded. 'There's enough there to feed the five thousand.'

'I don't want Matt thinking we don't provide a good enough service. He's already asked if he can add lunches to his deal.'

'Matt, eh? Already on first-name terms. I suppose you agreed to the lunches. Oh, Mum, we agreed, no midday meals. It's too much of a tie for you. You're already going to be working much too hard.'

'He only wants something like a sandwich, and he's offered to pay extra. He doesn't want to have to break into his day, finding somewhere to eat.'

'Honestly, Mum, you're hopeless. I expect you'll be trotting up with trays of coffee and a few home-made biscuits you just happened to have by. I think you're being a mug. He's obviously seen you're a soft touch.'

'I'm sorry you see it that way,' a deep male voice said from behind her. 'Sorry to interrupt. I'm just returning the tray and tea things. The home-made biscuits you happened to have in were delicious. I'm very grateful. You can always add it to my bill.'

Fliss swung round, ready to retort. She stopped, her mouth open, and wordlessly she stared at the vision. Her mother was right, though Greek god would be changed to drop-dead gorgeous in her own words. He was well over six feet tall, dark-haired and with the brooding expression described in every clichéd romance she'd ever read. He had lovely grey eyes and, well, he was simply beautiful, if you could have beautiful men.

'Handsome, I mean,' she whispered

almost out loud.

She gulped and immediately lost all track of any suitable words to use. Her mother was smiling and nodding like a demented daffodil in a breeze.

'This is my daughter, Fliss,' she was saying. 'She works for our local radio station, don't you, dear?'

'Yes,' Fliss managed to splutter in a voice that could never have made it into any sort of radio.

'Broadcasting, eh? I'm Matt Forbes. Matt to my friends. I hope you'll call me Matt.'

He held out his hand, a large but sensitive-looking hand.

'Sure. Matt it is,' Fliss said, beginning to recover some sort of equilibrium and still hanging on to his hand.

'And what is Fliss short for?' he asked in a voice that poured like thick chocolate.

'Felice,' her mother interrupted. 'We'd just been to France when she was on the way. It's such a pretty name. Can't think why she has to shorten it all the time.'

'Because everyone thinks Fliss is my name. Say it fast and Felice sounds like Fliss.'

'I shall say it slowly then.' Matt laughed.

I'm in love already, Fliss was thinking. For once, the winter was about to become the highlight of the year. Maybe she should resign from her job immediately and be available to provide endless trays of coffee and biscuits! She gave herself a mental shake. She was behaving like a moon-struck kid seeing a favourite pop star for the first time. She took a deep breath and managed a half-professional smile.

'So, Mr Forbes, Matt, have you written anything I might have read?'

'I'm not sure. I don't ever really know who likes my stuff. Hard to tell. Well, there's the tray. I'll go and get things sorted in my room. I mustn't take up any more of your valuable time. Dinner at seven you said, Mrs Crosby?'

'Sally. Please, call me Sally. Seven it

is, if that's convenient for you?'

'Fine.'

He nodded and went out of the kitchen.

'Even you have to admit our Mr Forbes is rather spectacular,' Sally Crosby said with a huge grin.

'He's all right, I suppose,' Fliss lied.

Her heart was still pounding and she felt slightly weak at the knees. Ridiculous, she told herself. He was only a man after all.

'I'd better go and change. What's on the menu for tonight?'

'Nothing complicated. I can manage on my own if you want to go out.'

' 'Course not. I'll be down after I've had a shower. Can't leave everything to you, can I? This is a partnership.'

'Whatever you say, dear,' her mother said with a knowing smile.

From her room, Fliss looked over the car park, towards the sea. It was going to be a rough night. The waves were already breaking high against the rocks and the wind was tearing against the shrubs in their usually pretty garden. She shivered, catching sight of movement in the car park. One of the two artist ladies was taking a bundle out of the boot of their little car. She was clutching a raincoat around herself but it was quite inadequate against the growing storm.

Fliss watched as the guest went back towards the building. The people-carrier had gone. Fancy Matt going out in this dreadful weather. Perhaps he had gone to collect something from the village, send a postcard to his children or something. A man like he was would surely have a glamorous wife and the requisite number of designer children.

She sighed. Local radio was hardly going to bring her the man of her dreams, whoever or whatever he was. Still, she was only twenty-five so hardly left on the shelf.

All the same, she certainly hadn't been making the best of herself lately. She wore simple shirts and either a long skirt or trousers for work. Sitting behind a desk most of the day, she didn't need to worry about the lower half. Visitors to the station saw only the top half. From now on, Matt Forbes would be seeing as much of her as possible and if that meant she needed to smarten herself up, then so be it.

'What are you like?' she asked her reflection. 'He's almost certainly married and with looks like his, he certainly won't be interested in a boring female like me. I'm nothing more than someone who answers the phone at the local radio station.'

Maybe she could do an interview with him, she thought. The mysterious writer who seeks solitude to complete his latest international bestseller. It would be the scoop of the year, but it was all fantasy, a foolish dream. She merely answered the phone and typed a few letters at the radio station. Her nearest claim to fame was that she handed out the mail to all the broadcasters each day and organised their phone messages. They were all quite normal, ordinary people without any pretentious nonsense among them. In fact, they were a pretty nice bunch on the whole. All the same, she could quite fancy doing a bit of actual broadcasting herself.

With a start, she realised she had been dreaming in front of her mirror for almost half an hour. It was high time she showered and changed and was helping with table laying. Her beauty treatment complete, she glanced out of the window again and saw that his vehicle was still absent from the car park. He'd be back for dinner, wherever he'd gone. She rushed down the stairs and bounced happily into the kitchen.

'Something smells spectacular,' she called out cheerfully to her mother. 'Shall I start on the tables or do you need help?'

'I'm fine. You sort out the tables. Matt says he'll use the dining room tonight, but in future, he'd prefer to eat in his room.'

'Bit stand-offish, isn't he?' Fliss said, desperately disappointed.

How could she get to know him if he was always locked away?

'Not good for him to stay shut away somewhere.'

'He says it's the only way not to get involved with all the other guests. Apparently people keep asking him to read their manuscripts and give free critics once they know he's a writer. They always think a writer can get them into the system, as well, or they know someone's daughter who can write beautifully. You know the sort of thing.'

'Sounds as though you had quite a chat with him,' Fliss said, a slight note of jealousy in her voice. 'When did you discover all this?'

'He was in here for a chat a little while ago. Shame you took so long over your shower. You could have been here to join in. He's very nice, isn't he?'

Suddenly, warning bells rang in Fliss's head. Her mother was doing all she could to push them together, not that she would have minded being pushed towards him but it was pretty demeaning for your own mother to be the one doing all the pushing. She laughed to herself. She had been fantasising for the last half hour, a stupid, romantic dream. As if anyone ever fell in love like that! Obviously, she had been reading too many romances lately. Her mother was staring at her.

'Well?' she demanded. 'I said, he's very nice, isn't he?'

'He's OK. Yes. He's pretty OK. Married and with a hoard of kids, no doubt, hence the reason for the enforced trip to finish his book.'

'Oh, you don't really think he's married, do you?'

Mrs Crosby stopped stirring a sauce for a moment and looked up at her daughter.

'Gosh, you look nice. Always did like you in that dress.'

There was a twinkle in her eye. Fliss knew at once that her mother had sussed her out. She rarely changed into anything other than jeans at this time of day, but she was wearing one of her better dresses in a deep orange that set off her colouring very well. She'd even put on some pale orange lipstick, something else almost unheard of lately. Amazing what an attractive man could do, however unavailable he proved to be.

' 'Course he's married. Else why does he drive a huge people-carrier?'

'I don't know what that is. Looked a perfectly ordinary car to me.'

'Take it from me, Mum, it's a people-carrier, designed for carrying lots of people. He's probably got at least two kids.'

'If you say so, dear. Now, are you going to do those tables?'

Fliss went into the dining room and began to set the cutlery carefully on the snowy white linen. They may only be doing reduced rate, winter stays but standards would be their usual level, especially on the table of Mr Matt

Forbes. Thoughtfully, she arranged the posy of flowers, wondering what his wife was really like. She glanced round the room. The log fire was burning cheerfully. The old beams and tiny, leaded windows added an air of mystery. At any moment, a smuggler could push his way in through the heavy, studded door. He would look warily around and demand to know if the excise men had been near.

'Is dinner nearly ready?' a female voice asked behind her.

Fliss gave a start and swung round to look at the new arrival, one of the old lady residents.

'I think so,' Fliss stammered, quite thrown by the intrusion.

'Only we wondered if it is possible to have a small sherry before we eat.'

'Of course,' Fliss replied with a smile. 'I'll get it immediately.'

'Thank you, dear, but I'll wait for my friend to come down. She won't be long. What a dreadful night. Thank goodness we're warm and safe inside.'

'Poor fishermen. Don't envy them on a night like this.'

'Oh, dear. Will they really have to go out in this weather?'

'We all want fresh fish on the menu. Someone has to catch it.'

Fliss wanted to excuse herself and see if her mother was ready for the guests but she didn't like to appear rude. As she heard footsteps on the stairs, all desire to help her mother disappeared as Matt came into the room.

'Evening,' he said as his commanding presence filled the room. 'May I have a whisky and American, please?'

'With ice?' Fliss squeaked.

Her normal voice had quite deserted her. She tried taking a deep breath to calm her stupid nerves.

'Thanks,' Matt said with a grin. 'Glad I'm not a fisherman tonight,' he said politely to include the other female guest.

'We were just saying the same thing,' the lady from Room Twelve replied. 'Are you staying for long, Mr er . . . '

'Matt Forbes,' he introduced himself.

'Couple of months maybe. Depends on how things go.'

'I'm Wyn Slater and the friend staying with me is Elaine Derricoat. We're trying to do some painting, you know. Such a very picturesque place, isn't it? Even in winter.'

'Your whisky,' Fliss said handing it to him, before he could reply. 'Do you want to start a tab or pay as you go?'

'Maybe a tab would be easier. I'm rarely organised enough to carry real money.'

'Ah, here's Elaine now. Do come along, dear. Mr Forbes has been keeping me entertained.'

Fliss had the sudden picture of some Agatha Christie type of country house party, with the characters assembling before the murder took place. She grinned at the thought. Maybe they ought to try murder weekends. Some places were very successful with them. This place was certainly perfect for such a thing. Maybe she could suggest it to her mother as another diversification. Elaine and Wyn could be the first

22

joint victims and she could then get on with her fantasising about Matt. He winked at her, as if reading her mind. She blushed and turned to grab the sherry bottle.

2

Towards the end of the meal, Fliss could see exactly why Matt would want to eat in his room in future. The two women were very sweet but very demanding in the conversation stakes. They reminded her of a pair of twittering birds, she realised. Poor Matt. She really should try to rescue him. He seemed to have steered clear of admitting he was a writer. Perhaps he wanted to keep it a secret for some reason.

'More coffee anyone? Liqueurs? Brandy?'

'Oh, dear, no. I'd be quite tipsy,' Wyn twittered. 'It's time for me to go to bed,' she insisted.

'Yes. We have an early start planned tomorrow,' Elaine added.

To Fliss's great relief, the pair of women got up and left the room.

'I should hit the hay myself,' Matt

announced and her heart sank. 'On the other hand, I could have that brandy you suggested. Perhaps you'd like to join me.'

'I'll join you for a coffee but I don't think I could cope with brandy, thanks. I'll get it for you. Shall we sit by the fire?'

'Ok.'

He moved to the comfortable leather sofa and sank into it. Fliss collected the drinks and came to join him.

'Let me take that,' he said, rising.

He put the tray in the centre of the table and indicated the sofa beside him. Fliss sank back with him. He felt warm and comfortable close to her. He smiled at her and handed her the coffee.

'Nice to see you relax. You must be exhausted. All this here after a day at work.'

'I'm used to it.'

'What about a social life?' he asked.

'What's that? I'm happy enough, really. Mum works pretty hard herself and I try to share the load.'

'And your father?'

'He died about four years ago. Things have been pretty tight since then, hence our winter rates instead of trying to run as an ordinary hotel through the winter.'

'Don't you have any restaurant trade? I'd have thought that you would, if tonight's meal is a sample of the standard of cooking here.'

'Odd ones. The whole country is rather in the doldrums at present.'

They chatted for half an hour. Not only was he gorgeous looking, he was also a very nice man indeed, easy to talk to and he had that special knack of always seeming interested in what the other person was saying.

'Sorry,' she said, realising she had been talking almost non-stop. 'I shouldn't be boring you with all this. You haven't had the chance to tell me anything about yourself.'

'Not a lot to tell.'

' 'Course there is. What about your wife, for instance? How does she feel about you being away for months on end?'

She closed her eyes, cursing her nosey nature. What a thing to ask. She never could keep out of anyone else's business.

'My wife?' Matt asked, looking surprised.

He was spared from answering by the arrival of Sally.

'I hope you enjoyed your dinner, Mr Forbes.'

'Matt, please. It was excellent. I was just telling Fliss here that I was surprised you don't have more local trade.'

The conversation moved on to safer ground, until at last, Matt excused himself and went up to his room.

'How did you get on with him, dear?' Sally asked anxiously.

'Fine, thanks. We were talking about his wife,' she said recklessly.

'Oh? He has got one, has he?'

'Mum, I told you he had.'

'And how many children?'

'You came in before we got round to that.'

'I see. Well, I'd better get the dishwasher going and get to bed. I'm whacked.'

'I'll see to it. You go to your room. 'Night, Mum. Love you lots.'

She gave her mum a hug and slumped down again, staring into the fire. She felt strange, as if she was on the verge of something new, something that was about to change her life.

'Ridiculous,' she muttered. 'Imagination and wishful thinking,' she tried to convince herself.

Fliss was up away to work long before any of the guests showed themselves the next morning. The storm the previous evening had left broken branches and leaves covering most of the roads. The rain had stopped but the winds still whipped the waves. She was used to it though and thought little of it. The car park at work was unusually empty. She had been listening to the local news as she drove in but had taken in very little.

' 'Morning,' she said cheerfully as she went into the cloakroom.

'You sound happy,' one of the female announcers said to her. 'You obviously haven't heard the news.'

'Sorry, what news?'

'Multiple pile-up on the A30. Trees have blown down and one landed on a car. Everyone's gone rushing over there and there's only a few of us here. The phone lines are going to be red hot, I expect.'

'I'd better get to it then,' Fliss replied. 'How dreadful. I thought I had the news on the car radio but my mind must have been drifting somewhere.'

'New man in your life, I expect.'

'I wish,' Fliss sighed.

She flicked a comb through her hair and went to the reception desk to take her usual place. The switchboard was already flashing as callers waited to be answered. Fortunately, there was no ringing sound as it might interrupt the live broadcasts. She began to answer the calls as they stacked up. Masses of people were phoning telling about traffic hold-ups and she passed them over to the road control centre. Some of them, she politely thanked and said they already had the information they were providing.

Other calls were asking for information and she desperately tried to catch up with the latest pieces of news on the screen in front of her. Stand-in people were keeping the music going and the interruptions became more and more frequent as the morning wore on. Reports varied between ten vehicles behind involved in the pile-up, right down to a tractor pushing a car off the road. The truth lay somewhere in between but so far, no-one had been killed. The radio had to try to give the most accurate news possible.

By lunchtime, the road was re-opened and things were getting back to normal. Fliss couldn't believe the variety in the so-called witness statements. It made her realise that one had reason to doubt almost everyone's words. She felt totally exhausted by the time she took her lunch-break, almost a full hour later than usual. She went into the town to find something to eat, simply to get away from the frenzied activity.

She wondered how things were back at Penmore Hotel and envied the tranquillity of the place. Was Matt typing away happily? The ladies off somewhere painting? Her mother would be sorting menus and ordering supplies. She gave a little sigh. She didn't really mind working at all. It made a change from the usual grind of the hotel routine.

'Hi,' Rick, one of the technicians from the radio, said. 'May I join you?'

Fliss nodded. He was a nice chap, around the same age as she was but totally wrapped up in the mechanics of his work.

'What a morning. Nothing like a spot of drama to get everyone going. At least no-one was killed, though I gather there were quite a few serious injuries.'

'But why do people want to exagger-ate?' Fliss asked.

'Human nature, I s'pose. News is only noticed if it's bad news.'

'I see what you mean.'

She glanced at her watch.

'I s'pose I'd better get back. Soon be time for the afternoon gardening slot. That always gets folk reaching for their phones.'

'Fliss, you wouldn't consider coming out with me one evening, would you? A drink or something? Film maybe?'

'Oh, I don't know,' Fliss replied, totally thrown by the request. 'We run a hotel, you know, Mum and I. I have to help out most evenings.'

'But you must have some time off, otherwise you'd go mad. Still, if you don't fancy the idea, don't worry. Just thought it might be nice.'

'Thanks for asking, Rick. It would be nice. Let me think about it.'

'Sure. Forget about it if you don't want to.'

Fliss left him eating his burger and

walked back across the little bridge. The wind was dying down a little though it was never as bad in the town. The tide was in, filling the river basin next to the studios. It looked quite picturesque with a few boats bobbing on the waves and the mud flats covered. The car park had filled up now, as the broadcasters came back from the scene of the accident.

She thought about Rick's invitation. She could scarcely remember the last time she'd been to the cinema and as for going out for a drink, well, living in a hotel, one waited for the drinkers to come to you. He was a nice enough chap but compared with Matt, a non-starter! She blushed. What a dreadful thing to think. How dare she compare anyone with anyone else? All the same, there was probably very little they had in common. Best not to start anything, she decided.

By the time she arrived home, she felt utterly drained. The highlight of the afternoon was taking a message into the

studio and Tony, the gardening programme host, actually introduced her,
live on air. She spoke her very first
words to the whole county. She smiled,
remembering the buzz she had felt, not
that a warning of severe driving
conditions was ever going to make her a
new career.

'Hi, Mum,' she called wearily.

'Hello, dear. Good day?'

'Lousy. Didn't you hear the news?'

'I've been far too busy.'

For the next few minutes, Sally
regaled her daughter with the various
doings of her day in which, it seemed,
Matt Forbes featured quite strongly.

'I hope you haven't been interrupting
his work.'

' 'Course not, silly. Just making him
feel at home. Being hospitable.'

'But he did say he wanted to work.
That's the whole reason for his being
here. Oh,' she remembered, 'you won't
have heard my very first live broadcast
then?'

'Oh, how exciting. Why didn't you

tell me you were going to be on? I'd have listened especially.'

Fliss changed into her jeans and a clean shirt for evening. She felt far too weary to make much effort. She set the tables and, listlessly, went back to the kitchen where she joined her mother.

'What you need is an evening out, my girl,' Sally informed her. 'Why don't you show Matt some of the night life?'

'Stop trying to matchmake, Mother. Anyway, what nightlife? It's Cornwall in the middle of winter, for goodness' sake.'

'I worry about you, dear. You don't show any interest in any young men. It's high time you were courting, thinking of the future.'

It was impossible to reason with her mother when she was in this mood. Fliss left her and hoped the guests would soon be down for dinner.

'Matt's tray is ready,' Sally called to her daughter. 'Will you take it up to his room?'

'Oh, I forgot he was doing that. What a pain.'

Fliss felt the sense of disappointment again. She had been hoping to try to get to know a little more about him but if he insisted on staying in his room, well, there was little chance of that. At least her mother was giving her the chance to take the food tray up to him. Better than nothing. She knocked on his door.

'Food, Matt.'

'Hang on,' he said and she heard him moving across the room to the door. 'Wow, that looks good,' he said appreciatively.

'But you can't see anything yet. Your meal's covered with another plate.'

'Maybe I wasn't just meaning the food,' he said with a soft smile.

'If that was meant as a compliment, thank you. But I'm hardly dressed for compliments. I've had a lousy day and feel quite shattered.'

'Then you should have a glass of wine with me,' he offered.

Fliss smiled. Normally, she would have jumped at the chance but he needed to eat his meal. It wouldn't be fair to him.

'I don't want to spoil your meal. I thought you wanted to eat in your room to save having to make conversation.'

'You're different, Fliss. Felice. I'd enjoy your company. Why don't you bring your meal up here and we can eat together?'

'I couldn't do that. What on earth would my mother think?'

'OK. Compromise. Bring your dessert up and have it with me and bring a coffee pot.'

He smiled again and she felt herself become quite weak at the knees. He actually sounded as if he wanted her company.

'Well, if you're sure.'

'I'm positive. What red-blooded male wouldn't want a beautiful, young woman to keep him company?'

'You're simply too good to be true,' she blurted out. 'What's the catch?'

'Is there one?' he countered.

'Usually. A handsome man like you

shouldn't be on his own in a remote country hotel. Perhaps you're on the run or something.'

'Handsome, eh? That's surely a point in my favour. I'll expect you and my pudding and coffee in about half an hour. Deal?'

'Deal,' she murmured.

Her mother could hardly wait.

'Are you going to go out with him?'

'Mum,' she groaned, 'I've simply taken his meal to him. What's the matter with you? You're not usually so obsessed with marrying me off to the first taker. I'm going to have coffee with him. All right? Will that do for now?'

Her mother said nothing and smiled enigmatically. She busied herself with the dessert tray for Matt, setting it for two. Fliss went to clear the ladies' plates and fended off an array of questions about the other missing guest. Maybe he had a good point about sharing meals with other people.

'Tell me about the radio station,' he asked once she joined him.

Fliss began to answer him and was soon in full swing. Suddenly, she stopped.

'What is it about you?' she asked. 'You always get me rabbiting on about myself and yet you never tell me anything. I don't even know what sort of books you write.'

'I'm not sure whether you'd like them. I expect you are far too busy to read much.'

She coloured slightly. He did have a point. The extent of her reading was usually limited to a few magazines and the rest was romance.

'You're right. I don't have much time. Still, you never know.'

'I have an assumed name, of course. Helps me to remain anonymous. Say, your mother said you might be willing to show me something of the area. The night life was actually what she said.'

He laughed. Even his teeth were perfect, Fliss noticed.

'My mother has a very wild imagination. There's not a great deal of night life in this area. I'm not really into the club scene and I get enough chance to socialise behind the bar here to want to spend too much time in pubs.'

'I can understand that. So, maybe there are concerts or something you might like to go to.'

'Oh, don't get me wrong, there is plenty going on really. I just always seem to be busy here and never get round to going out much.'

'Sounds like your mum was right. You do need taking out of yourself. You know, I never expected there to be someone like you here. I had the vision of a small hotel with a comfortable, middle-aged couple looking after me. Instead I find I am being looked after by someone who is the perfect mother substitute and her lovely daughter. We only need the smugglers to call in to complete the romance.'

'Very Daphne du Maurier. Could do with some swashing and buckling around here. You might be able to help me. I was thinking about starting one of those murder weekends. You know the sort of thing, when everyone dresses up and has a part to play and helps solve the mystery.'

'Could be good. Where do I fit in?'

'Well, as a writer, you could maybe write us a script.'

'Oh, just like that? I'm not quite that sort of writer. But there are companies who could come and run it for you. All you'd have to do would be to organise the meals and guests. It could work.'

'I suppose I just telephone and order it, do I?' she said with a hint of sarcasm.

'I'm sure you could find someone in an area like this,' he said with a laugh. 'Hey, come on, I was teasing,' he said as a flicker of irritation crossed her face. 'Seriously, I can probably find out something for you.'

'Great. Thanks. Now, I'd better go and help Mum. Thanks for the chat.'

'Thanks for the company. And I would like you to go out with me one evening, if there's no-one else around to be jealous.'

Fliss gave him an enigmatic smile as she collected the tray.

'We'll see what happens, shall we?' she said softly.

She was getting used to him, she decided. Beneath the devastating looks and the overwhelming feeling his presence provoked, he was just another bloke. It must be a bit like falling seriously for some pop star. The presence and charisma must be over-whelming until one could get used to simply being with the famous person. Must be tricky to sort out real feelings, she speculated.

'Good-night, Fliss,' he said, holding the door open for her.

She was carrying the tray and turned slightly to edge it through the door. To her amazement, he leaned over and kissed her cheek as she passed.

'Matt,' she protested, 'what do you think you're doing?'

'Sorry. It suddenly seemed like the

right thing to do. I wanted very much to kiss you but thought a peck on the cheek was harmless.'

'I don't know you, Matt. And your wife? What would she think about a harmless peck on the cheek? Someone else's cheek!'

'Leave any wife of mine out of this,' he snapped. 'Sorry, I made a mistake. Please accept my apology. It won't happen again.'

Trying to look angry, she left the room.

3

Fliss felt her cheeks growing redder. He hadn't even denied he had a wife, she realised. Never could she remember feeling so attracted to a man. She was probably being totally naïve and stupid, but she fancied Matt Forbes strongly. Married or not, he was having a devastating effect on her.

By the time she reached the kitchen, she was a fiery red. Luckily, her mother had left. She was probably sitting in front of the TV, wondering how things were progressing with her and Matt. Dear, sweet Mum, Fliss thought fondly. Pushing her one and only daughter straight into the arms of an obviously, married man — she'd probably be horrified if she realised.

She stacked the dirty dishes in the machine and turned it on. She glanced round and switched the light off as she left. She gave a shiver. It was turning very cold. Perhaps the heating was a bit low. She felt the radiator in the dining room but it was as hot as ever. She locked the front door and went upstairs to their small flat.

'You in there, Mum?' she called softly outside the sitting room.

She pushed the door open gently so she didn't disturb her mother.

'Oh, Fliss. I did so want to watch that film but must have nodded off.'

Fliss grinned. Her mum was always doing that. At least this time, she wasn't demanding that Fliss should tell her the plot to catch up on what she'd missed.

'Typical,' she said fondly. 'I've locked the door for the night. I assume everyone's in.'

'I guess so. You decided not to go out with Matt then?'

'Not tonight. It's much too wild out there, and it's turned really cold. Wouldn't be surprised if we got some snow.'

'I doubt it. The sea always keeps us

warmer than inland. Are you coming to watch something with me?'

'I'll see the news and then I wouldn't mind an early night.'

They watched the news together then Fliss took herself off to bed. Her mind was in rather a turmoil. Matt's peck on the cheek had left her feeling confused. He obviously liked her and had sought out her company, yet it seemed as if he must have a wife somewhere, as he had never denied it. But why had he come to this remote hotel? Why didn't she want to be with him? She could think of no satisfactory answers. She snuggled down beneath her duvet and listened to the roaring of the wind and sea.

The windows rattled in their ancient frames. She wondered just how long they could possibly continue to run the business. Maybe they should give up and try to sell the place next year. She felt weary at the thought of another season of struggling to make ends meet. Since Dad died, nothing had been straightforward. Her mother was beginning to show definite signs of strain. Whatever lay ahead, it was pointless trying to think about any serious moves until the spring. She turned over and tried to shut out the noises of the storm. She drifted off to sleep eventually.

It was around three-thirty when the huge bang echoed through the building. Fliss shot up and reached for the bedside light. Nothing happened. She fumbled in the dark for the torch she knew was somewhere in the bedside cabinet and shivered. It was even colder than when she had gone to bed. She grabbed a sweater and pulled it over her pyjamas. The torch was not to be found, so she felt her way out of her room and along the dark corridor. The power had obviously failed.

'Fliss?' her mother called from along the corridor.

'Yes. I think the power's off. Maybe a fuse has blown.'

'I think it's the storm. Probably blown a cable down or something. We'd

47

better go down and look. Haven't you got your torch?'

'No. Can't find it. I'll use one of the oil lamps when I get downstairs.'

She groped her way along the corridor and down the stairs. The room was intensely black with no reflected light from anywhere outside. At least that must mean the power was off everywhere around, and not just in the hotel. Even that was some small comfort as it was unlikely to be something that would cost huge amounts of money to repair.

She found some matches and a candle on one of the tables, and went to the mantelpiece to pick up one of the old-fashioned oil lamps, kept to look atmospheric but now having a real purpose. The room looked as it should, though slightly spooky in the flickering light. She went into the kitchen, still curious to find the cause of the crash that had awoken her.

She stopped just in time. The kitchen floor was covered in broken glass. She had bare feet and would have been badly cut had she walked in there. She held the lamp high and saw the broken pane of glass. The whole window had somehow shattered and flung itself to the floor. All the stainless steel units had shards of broken glass gleaming in the lamplight and the tiled floor was a minefield. The cause of the incident was not yet apparent.

'What's wrong?' a male voice asked behind her. 'I heard a colossal bang and the lights don't work.'

'Tell me about it,' Fliss said grimly.

'Look at you with nothing on your feet. You'll catch your death of cold.'

'Not to mention severe cuts,' she replied.

He glanced into the kitchen.

'What on earth happened? Is it a lightning strike or something?'

'I really don't know. It's almost as if someone chucked a great boulder through the window.'

'I can't see anything like that. It would have to be lying on the floor if it was. Besides, that window is quite some height off the ground.'

The hotel was built partly into the side of the cliff and the upper rooms were at ground level only at the back of the building. The front, where the kitchen was, had a steep drop outside the window.

'Look, you'd better go and put some shoes on, and some more clothes. It's absolutely freezing,' he said.

Fliss lit a couple more candles and found a torch behind the small bar. She went back upstairs and pulled on jeans, thick socks and her trainers. Halfway through dressing, her mother groped her way along the corridor.

'What was it, dear?' she asked.

'The kitchen window has been smashed and the power's off.'

'How do you mean, the kitchen window? What's wrong with it?'

'It's currently lying all over the kitchen floor,' she tried to joke feebly. 'It's OK. Matt's down there, too, and I just came to put on some clothes and shoes. You stay where you are. I'll try and sort something out.'

Matt had already found a dustpan and brush and was busily shovelling broken glass into a bucket. It was a large, double glazed window and the amount of glass was quite incredible.

'Have you got some boxes or something? This bucket's full and I've barely started.'

'There should be some in the back,' she told him, walking carefully past the glass.

The wind was howling through the opening, making the room even colder. There were even a few flurries of snow blasting their way in. It made the clearing up very much more difficult. After half an hour of hard sweeping and moving boxes, the worst of the glass had been picked up.

'We ought to try and cover the gap with something,' Matt suggested. 'Otherwise, the wet will damage the electrical stuff. Have you got any boards or large pieces of wood?'

Fliss tried to think. They had masses of polythene but that would be useless against this wind.

'I know. There's a table tennis table out in the shed. We put it up on the lawn for the kids to play with in summer. That might do it.'

Matt looked doubtful. Handling a large table in the wind and in the dark was going to prove quite a task.

'If you say so. Let's take a look, anyhow.'

They tried to open the rear door and it was practically wrenched out of their hands. The blasts of air were finding every way they could to get into the kitchen. It was so bad, they could barely stand and both were soaked in seconds as the snow and hail were driven into their clothing by the wind.

'Tranquil Cornwall,' Matt said through clenched teeth. 'Quite a selling point, wasn't it?'

But Fliss could hear nothing. She was intent on pulling the shed door open. She flashed the torch into the lean-to and showed Matt the large table. If they could only manage to pull it through the storm, it would at least block the wind a bit. They'd have to push heavy units against it to stop it blowing over.

'Come on then,' he bellowed. 'Let's see what we can do.'

By six o'clock, they were sitting by candlelight and oil lamp in the dining room. They were exhausted and Sally was busily trying to organise something hot, courtesy of the log fire she had lit in the old grate. It was still freezing cold. The power was still showing no signs of being restored and the noise of howling wind funnelled round the table that was resting against the broken window. There was a chilled, spooky air to the place.

'I'm so sorry,' Sally kept apologising. 'You have been most kind, Matt, but you shouldn't be asked to help in this way.'

'Nonsense. You couldn't have managed on your own, though I must admit, Fliss is as tough and resourceful as anyone I've met, quite a gal.'

Fliss grimaced at his sudden pseudo-American accent. She retaliated with her own exaggeration of a Cornish accent.

'It's the way they breed 'em down 'ere. Tough as the land they live in,' she said then returned to her normal voice and said, 'Any luck with that kettle, Mum? I'm getting desperate.'

'Almost there. I simply don't know how on earth we're going to manage for breakfast, though. I can hardly fry bacon here. Oh, dear, this really is the last straw. How on earth are we going to pay for the window to be fixed, on top of everything else? It'll cost a fortune, by the time they've raised scaffolding and everything.'

'Surely your insurance will pay,' Matt suggested.

'Insurance?' Sally said wearily.

'Sure. Don't tell me you haven't got insurance. You must have, to run as a hotel.'

' 'Course we have,' Fliss chimed in, then she bit her lip. 'Assuming you sent off the cheque, Mum. It was due for renewal last month.'

There was a silence. Sally looked uncomfortable.

'I did send it but the bank wouldn't clear the cheque. I did instruct them to pay it as soon as the credit was there. I simply never checked to see if they did.'

An air of gloom descended on the dim room. Fliss shivered. She could see everything slipping out of control. It was madness to try and run this hotel. It needed a fortune spending on it and twice as many staff as they could afford. They were living on a dream, and it was turning into a worst nightmare.

4

You mean to say, you haven't got any insurance?' Matt spluttered incredulously as Sally's words took effect.

'Oh, Mum. Why didn't you tell me about it?' Fliss asked.

'I didn't want you to worry any more than you already are. I know I'm a fool and I feel just as bad about it as you do, probably far worse in fact.'

Sally looked near to tears. Fliss got up and put her arms round her.

'I'm not blaming you, but for heaven's sake, tell me about anything like that in future. In the meantime, we simply have to get the window fixed, whatever the cost. We can't function without it, can we?'

The hot coffee was finally produced, but brought small comfort to the trio. As daylight began to show, they felt more able to begin to make plans. Fliss phoned the electricity company, who assured her the power would be restored by nine o'clock. If the ladies insisted on a cooked breakfast, they could either wait or by some means, Sally would manage something on the tiny primus stove that Fliss had dug out of the shed.

'I'll start with hot porridge. That'll warm everyone up,' Sally decided.

Despite her lack of sleep, Fliss was expected at work on time and she would just have to cope somehow. If nothing else, she reflected gloomily, she would need to earn a decent salary if only to pay for things like broken windows. Once at work, she called the local glazier, who agreed to go and measure the window and construct a temporary replacement as an emergency.

When she finally found time to call her mother, just before lunch-time, she learned that the power was still off. The other bad news was that the glazier had said it would be at least the next day before they could return to fix the window as the height of it made it impossible to reach without scaffolding and that would take some time to erect safely.

'And did they mention a price?' Fliss asked in trepidation.

'You don't want to know, dear,' Sally replied. 'But, as you said, we can't function without it. I phoned the insurance and guess what? If they'd got the cheque a day earlier, we'd have been covered. The bank assured me it was sent off as I requested but they claimed it hadn't arrived in time. Oh, how I hate insurance brokers.'

'I'll call in and see them after work,' Fliss promised.

Somehow, the personal approach just had to work.

'I shall be firm with them and tell them to pay up, or we shall be looking elsewhere in future. You do know they have special courses in how to get out of paying up?'

'Don't be silly, dear, but you can

always try. We need the financial help badly enough, don't we?'

The radio station was inundated with calls for most of the day. It seemed that the entire county had been hit by the storms and all the callers had complaints and information about the damage. Fliss was totally exhausted by the end of the day and felt like collapsing into her bed rather than going to do battle with the insurance agents. But she knew she had to go.

After a long and frustrating discussion, she finally reached some sort of compromise. They finally agreed to pay part of the cost of the window, as a gesture of good will. The fitting and cost of scaffolding would be the client's responsibility. It was certainly better than nothing but still left them with a huge bill to face. She arrived home late, hungry and tired. Candles still flickered inside the windows and Fliss groaned. Still no electricity? She pushed her way into the kitchen and found her mother stirring a pan of soup on the little primus that was miraculously still working. Along the central table were ranged various pots and pans, each containing something cooked and steaming gently.

'I'm enjoying the challenge,' Sally said. 'I'm doing a hot meal despite everything. Poor things all need something hot after the dreadful day. I wouldn't be surprised if everyone decided to leave after this. But, as they're still hanging on, I thought I should try to see what I could come up with.'

'You're amazing, Mum,' Sally whispered.

'And you're exhausted. Why don't you go and take a nice hot bath?'

'Is there hot water, by some miracle?' Fliss asked innocently.

'Oh, no,' Sally remembered. 'I've been fantasising about having our own generator all afternoon. That would have solved everything. Still, the electricity board reckon they are on the case and won't be much longer.'

'Like they promised at nine o'clock this morning?' Fliss reminded her. 'I'll go and nag them once more.'

As she crossed to the phone, there was a loud crackle and light flooded the place. The kettle began to boil and sounds of appliances returning to life made both women smile.

'There, you see? They've heard of my reputation and the mere threat of a call from me was enough to get them going.'

Sally went to the cooker and turned on the oven. As she did so, there was another pop and everything went off again. She cursed as she fumbled for matches to re-light the candles.

'Now I really shall phone,' Fliss said snappily. 'If the threat alone was enough the first time, just guess what the real thing can do.'

In the event, it achieved nothing more than an opportunity for Fliss to vent some of her temper. All the engineers were apparently working flat out and it was now a power failure at the sub station.

As she slammed the phone down, there was a knock on the kitchen door.

'May I come in?' Matt asked. 'What's going on?'

Fliss told him the latest news, including her visit to the insurers.

'Well done. That's something at least.'

'You didn't tell me that,' Sally accused her. 'The insurance company was adamant that they weren't paying anything to me.'

'Just shows the power of a pretty face and a bit of persuasion,' Matt said with a grin at Fliss. 'I did say you were quite a gal.'

'That sounds remarkably sexist to me,' Fliss began but gave up and grinned instead — things were stressful enough.

'I don't know what on earth you are managing to cook Sally, but it smells wonderful.'

'I'm just about ready, I think. How about calling the ladies down? They must be thoroughly fed up by now. Weather too bad for anything and no heat or light all day. Give them some complimentary drinks to try and put them in a better mood.'

Fliss climbed the stairs to the visitors' rooms and tapped on their doors.

'Dinner is almost ready. Would you like to come down for a drink with us?' she asked politely.

'Is it any warmer down there? It's been terrible up here. I've spent the whole day reading, wrapped in the duvet,' Wyn Slater moaned.

'There's a good fire going and Mum's prepared a hot meal. Not sure how she's done it on a single primus stove, but she has.'

'Very well. We'll be down in a minute,' Elaine said.

'Tell me, dear, is the lovely Mr Forbes joining us?'

'Perhaps,' Fliss said cautiously. 'I'm not sure what his plans are.'

'Such a handsome man, isn't he?'

Fliss smiled as she returned to the dining room. So, Matt was setting even their hearts a-flutter, was he? She didn't blame them. After all, her own heart had made a few unpredicted leaps itself lately. In the cosy dining room, the log fire was roaring away and candles and oil lamps gave an atmosphere of timelessness. If she half closed her eyes, she could imagine old sailors sitting round the fire, swapping yarns of seafaring and smuggling. She could almost smell the smoke of their pipes and the scent of old rum. The wind was still howling around the ancient stones and some of the windows rattled. They'd have to be on their guard, in case the customs men arrived!

'Ho! Ho, my buxom wench. And what can I be a-gettin' for you?' a man's voice said.

She almost fell flat in fright.

'Matt! You scared me half to death. And I'm not a buxom wench, thank you very much. No, I was just imagining the old sailors who must once have sat round this fire.'

'I know,' Matt said simply. 'It showed on your face. You looked as if you were from another world, another time, except for the jeans, of course. They're totally twenty-first century. As I said, what can I get you to drink?'

'That should be my job,' Fliss protested feebly.

'Well, let's just say I've been taken on as temporary staff for one night.'

'Glass of wine then, red, please. Oh, and your fan club is on its way down. I assume you are having dinner down here tonight?'

'And you are joining me. Your mother insisted that she wants you out of the way while she's juggling pans and primus stoves.'

'OK, thanks,' Fliss agreed, gratefully.

It was easier not to argue and at least Matt's company might stop her from falling asleep in the soup.

'I'd better lay the tables.'

'Done,' Matt told her. 'At least, it's done the way I lay tables. You'd probably better check the ladies' table.'

The meal was a great success. The two ladies fluttered around Matt, if not physically, then verbally. He would say nothing about his writing, however much they probed. As with Fliss, he was reticent to give away even the smallest details of his work.

'Are you very famous then?' Elaine asked. 'You must use a pen name. I've certainly never heard of Matt Forbes. Do tell us what it is. It would be such a thrill to know someone famous was sitting at the very next table.'

Matt smiled enigmatically and said nothing.

'Are your books about birds?' Wyn asked bluntly. 'Because if so, my friend and I do paint, you know. You might like to look at some of our work, just in case you need illustrations of any kind.'

'Nothing to do with birds,' Matt replied with a wry grin. 'I'm sorry, but I'm feeling utterly exhausted and I must go to bed before I disgrace myself and fall asleep. You will excuse me?'

He rose from the table and Fliss smiled at him as he was leaving. She picked up the plates from the table and followed him.

'No coffee this evening?' she called softly after him.

'I thought you might like to bring it to my room for me, unless you have other plans.'

'I'm not sure it's a good idea,' she began, blushing at the memory of the peck on the cheek of the previous evening and the effect it had on her.

He had thought it quite natural but he had never once denied that he had a wife. Why was he so cagey about it, if he really wasn't married? There must be some reason and a wife had to be the only possible explanation. Taken all round, he was an extremely secretive man. Perhaps he truly did have something to hide.

'Well?' he asked again, interrupting her thoughts.

'I don't think I should. It isn't really the thing to do, visit a man's bedroom quite so often, I mean. I have my reputation to consider.'

'Whatever you think. I didn't have you down as a prude, though. I thought it would be nice to have a chat, on our own, without our friends listening to everything we're saying. Please, Fliss, won't you stay awhile?'

Fliss yawned. She felt utterly exhausted and all she really wanted to do was to collapse.

'Look, I'm sorry, Matt, but everything else apart, I really do need some sleep. I've had a very hectic day and after being up half the night, I'm practically asleep on my feet.'

He smiled and nodded his agreement.

'I wasn't thinking. Sorry. I did have a long snooze during the afternoon. You must be exhausted. I'll say good-night.'

Fliss went into the kitchen and found her mother sitting on a stool.

'You look done in, Mum. Have you eaten anything yourself? It was a terrific meal under the circumstances.'

'I had some soup. I really don't want much else. Never do when I'm cooking.'

'Leave this lot till tomorrow. The power must be on again soon. We can stack it in the dishwasher and run it in the morning. I'm off to bed, too, before I drop.'

She gave her mum a hug and went up to her room. She glanced at Matt's door as she passed. It was tempting to knock and say good-night, but she knew it could be opening a real can of worms. She whispered a silent good-night and went into her own room. How she longed for a hot shower and warm bed. Instead, she pulled on some thick, clean socks and went to bed in her jeans and sweater.

The tapping at her door fitted so nicely into her dream that she ignored it completely. Then it continued for a bit too long and she began to come to.

'Fliss? Wake up,' Matt's voice called. 'Quickly. There seems to be something burning downstairs.'

She shot out of bed and tried to find a dressing-gown. Then she realised she was still dressed and slipped on some shoes. She felt slightly dizzy from her rapid awakening and bumped into the door before opening it. Matt had already gone down and she rushed after him. In the kitchen, smoke was beginning to fill the room.

'What is it?' she asked as she went in, coughing from the fumes.

'Dunno. Seems to be coming from the primus.'

He shone his torch towards the worktop.

'Yes. Your mum must have left the soup on. Odd. That was the first course and she produced lots of other things after that.'

'She did have some soup herself. She must have forgotten to turn it off.'

'It's just about out now. I think the stove must be running out of fuel.'

'It's not like her to leave something on like that. She's meticulous about turning everything off before leaving it. Well, if it's just a burned pan, that's the least of our worries.'

Matt had covered the pan with a lid, trapping the smoke inside.

'No real harm done.'

'Thank goodness you smelled it or who knows what could have happened. Good job for us that you were staying here.'

He grinned, a boyish smile that made him look younger.

'I'd better go back to bed or I'll still be tired in the morning. Thanks again, Matt.'

'Don't mention it. Look, Fliss. There's something I need to say to you. About my . . . er . . . wife.'

'Not now, Matt. This isn't the time for long confessions. I really do need to sleep.'

She left him and went back to her room. Besides, she was thinking, the last thing I want to hear now is about your wife, Matt Forbes. If I have to fall in love with you, it might be easier not to know about the woman you love.

'Fall in love?' she whispered out loud. 'What drivel am I thinking now? Lack of sleep must be affecting my state of mind.'

Fiercely, she snapped off her torch and rolled back into bed. An hour later, she was still tossing, turning and trying to find some way to be comfortable. Just before five o'clock, there were a number of rumblings and creaks. She saw her bedside radio clock light and realised the power was back at last. At least she could have a hot shower and they could begin to get back to normal. She could hear noises from downstairs and knew that some of the kitchen machines, dishwasher and water heater, were beginning to run. The radiators creaked as warmth crept along the pipes.

Sally knocked at her door around seven and came in to wake Fliss.

'You still sleeping, dear?' she asked, pulling back the curtains. 'The power's back, thank heavens. I really don't think I could have coped with another day like yesterday. Nightmare.'

'You did really well, Mum. I'm proud of you.'

By the time she went down, the tantalising smells of fresh coffee and bacon were filling the air. The ruined soup pan was soaking in the sink.

'I can't think what happened to that,' Sally said. 'It looks as if it was left on the heat but I'm sure I turned off the primus. And the soup pan was on the draining board when I left. Did someone else come down and heat it up, I wonder. Maybe Matt needed something hot to eat and didn't like to ask.'

'It wasn't Matt. In fact, he came to fetch me when he smelled the burning.'

'But I distinctly remember putting the pan ready to wash up this morning. How odd. I must have thought I'd done and didn't.'

Fliss looked troubled. She hoped her mother wasn't beginning to be forgetful. She had always been so alert. She ate the breakfast her mother placed in front of her and said little.

'Thanks, Mum,' she said as she finished eating. 'That was great. Now, I'd better go and shower and get off to the fun factory.'

She met Matt on her way back to her

room and said a stiff good morning.

'Thanks again for your help,' she said. 'Sorry, I have to dash or I'll be late for work.'

'That's OK,' he said as she fled to her room.

He looked after her and sighed. He really needed time to talk to her.

5

When Fliss arrived safely at the radio station, she was met by one of the producers as soon as she stepped indoors.

'Thank heavens you're here. Sarah-Anne has called in sick and we're hoping Dave Mac will come in early to cover his own and her programmes. But it's going to take him some time to get here. I need you to stand in for at least half an hour. I'm sure you know roughly what to do. I'll help with what I can. It's mostly phone-ins at this time of day so you don't have to do anything with the music side. OK? Go straight through to the studio and I'll catch up with you.'

'R-right,' Fliss muttered suddenly going cold.

She discovered her legs were shaking and she realised she was suffering from stage fright!

'I don't think I can,' she squeaked but there was no-one to hear her.

She pushed through the door and into the corridor leading to the studio. The heavy door was almost too much for her to push open in her present state of terror.

'And I once thought I wanted to do live broadcasts,' she muttered.

'Oh, and here is the lovely Fliss,' Tom said, the morning programme announcer. 'I understand she's coming to take charge of you all this morning. I tell you, Cornwall, it's exciting here this morning. You were expecting to hear Sarah-Ann, weren't you? Instead, you are about to have the pleasure of a new lady on the team, Fliss Crosby. She's the lady you will have spoken to first, if you've ever phoned in. Say good morning, Fliss.'

He handed the microphone over to her and, trembling, she managed to mumble, 'Good morning, Cornwall.

'We're going over to the newsroom now and I'll leave you in Fliss's capable hands for the next programme. 'Bye.'

Fliss grinned at Tom and took over his seat. She desperately needed something to drink.

'Have fun, love,' he told her. 'Good of you to step in. I thought I was going to be here for the duration. I have an appointment with a cup of coffee right now. Just make sure you don't say anything you might regret if this switch is down. 'Bye. Good luck.'

'Thanks,' Fliss stammered, staring at the complex array in front of her.

She had been shown the general working of the studio and had watched so many times when she brought the announcements through. But now that she seemed to be in sole charge, it all looked far too complex. She clamped the headphones over her ears and was relieved to hear Julie's comforting voice immediately.

'OK, Fliss, introduce yourself. Tell them something about you as a person, if you like, and then we'll cue in the phone calls. It isn't that different from what you're doing on the front desk every day.'

'Except that I'm not on air when I'm on the front desk.'

'You'll be fine. OK. Five-four-three-two-one, go.'

'Good morning, Cornwall. Fliss Crosby here, standing in for Sarah-Anne. She's feeling rather out of sorts today and I'm sure you all join with me in wishing her well. I hope I won't press too many wrong switches and that you will forgive me if I do. OK. We have the lines open for your calls.'

Suddenly, Fliss was happy with what she was doing. After her first hesitant words, the nerves disappeared. This was it. This was exciting and exactly what she wanted to do with her life. Her training as a receptionist and her secretarial work had given her good communication skills. She was incredibly lucky to have been given this chance to discover the thrill of live radio. A chance in a million, she knew it. Hundreds of people would give their eye teeth to be in her shoes. It was a simple case of being in the right place at the right time.

When Dave Mac finally arrived, Fliss realised to her surprise that she felt very disappointed. He put his head round the door and mouthed that he would be ready in a few minutes. She nodded and continued to speak to her caller. Ten minutes later, she was making coffee in the little kitchen above the studios.

'Well done,' Julie told her. 'You're a natural. We'll have to call on you again. If you can go back to the desk once you've had a break, I think Rick will be delighted.'

'Rick?' Fliss echoed. 'But he's a technician.'

'Yes, and don't we know it. He's made a total muddle of your wonderfully simple system at the desk!'

'Won't be long then,' Fliss assured her. 'You know, I really enjoyed that. I'll be happy to stand in whenever you like.'

She was glowing with pride and pleasure as she took up her normal seat at the reception desk. As soon as Rick's muddle was sorted out, she called her mother.

'Oh, Fliss, I was so proud of you.'

'You heard it then? My début broadcast?'

'Matt heard you and came rushing down to tell me. You did do well. But why didn't you tell us you were going to be on?'

'I didn't know, until I got here. Anyhow, glad you heard it and I'll see you later. Have to go now.'

She hung up, leaving her mother still enthusing about the broadcast. She felt pleased that Matt had heard it, too. Not that it made any difference, but all the same, she felt gratified that she was seen as a real person and not just a part of the hotel. The rest of the day sped by and soon she was ready to go home. Hopefully, tonight would be free of dramas and disasters, especially those happening in the middle of the night.

She looked forward to a night of uninterrupted sleep. But when she arrived home, things were not looking promising.

'I don't believe it,' Sally was saying as she tussled with the dishwasher. 'There seems to be something stuck at the back of it.'

'Let me look,' Fliss said with a sigh.

So much for the quiet cup of tea and half an hour with her feet up. She peered into the machine and could see something at the base, near the drain hole. She tugged and a length of fabric appeared. It had wound itself round the spray, stopping it from moving. Undoubtedly, it would have burned the motor if it hadn't been found.

'Now, how on earth did that get in there?' she asked her mother.

'I really have no idea. I'd never put any clothes into the machine. You know I wouldn't.'

'You didn't try to clean it out and leave it in there?'

'Oh, Fliss, I'm not totally stupid. I

may forget a few things occasionally, but I'm not quite senile yet.'

'No, of course you're not,' Fliss assured her.

All the same, she pondered over some of the things that had been going wrong lately. In fact, she realised, ever since she had been away from the hotel each day. Maybe there was some medical problem developing in Sally's mind, which neither of them had noticed when Fliss was at home.

Several more irritating problems occurred over the next few days. A bird got in the kitchen when the door was left open. There was a wire screen which usually prevented this, but that, too, had been propped open. The bird had left a trail of damage and mess to be cleared. Then one of the rubbish skips somehow managed to slide down the car park and fall over the cliff, on to the beach below. It was fortunate that there weren't any holidaymakers around at the time or there might have been a serious injury.

Then the freezer was turned off one night and everything defrosted. It was a double blow after the long power cut had spoiled the contents only the previous week. Fortunately, the insurance for the freezer was a separate policy and was fully paid up to date. However, whether or not it covered such a silly mistake, and for the second claim so soon, was yet to be seen.

'I really am getting worried about my mother,' Fliss confided in Matt after dinner one evening. 'She's getting very forgetful and leaving small jobs unfinished and switches turned off. The soup-pan fire was the first of a whole string of things that have happened lately.'

'Maybe someone's trying to put you out of business,' Matt suggested.

'Don't be daft,' she said before she could stop herself. 'Why would anyone want to do that?'

'Maybe someone's trying to make you sell this place, at a cheap price.'

'You write mystery novels, I take it?'

she said sarcastically.

'It was just a thought, a possibility. You're probably right. Who'd want to buy it?'

When she told her mother of Matt's suggestion, she laughed.

'I can't think of anyone who'd be daft enough to want to buy it. But all the same, I know I'd hate anyone else to have it, wouldn't you? It's been your home all your life, practically. Such happy memories, too.'

'Yes. Well, yes, same for me. I'm going to have a shower and then I'll help with dinner.'

She met Matt on her way to her room.

'How would you like to go out to dinner this evening?' he asked.

'Mum would be devastated. She's in full cooking mode, right at this very moment.'

'Of course. Well, maybe we could have a drink later? You can introduce me to some of the local night life.'

'Actually, there is a band on at one of

the pubs tonight. Someone at work told me about it. I'd quite like to catch that. Don't know if it's your sort of music though.'

'I don't think I have a sort of music,' Matt replied. 'I'm game for anything. I've been working hard these last few days and I need a break.'

'See you later then,' she said, trying hard not to let him see the blush of pleasure that swept over her.

She went into her room and hugged herself. She was going to spend an evening with this gorgeous man. It would do her good to go somewhere different, especially with a good-looking male in tow. She bit her lip. He had tried on a number of occasions to talk about his wife and each time she had stopped him. She didn't want to know about her. Somehow, if Fliss didn't know about her, she wouldn't seem like a real person.

It was a very innocent relationship between her and Matt and hopefully, it could never be a real problem. All the same, she was playing with fire in her own heart, she tried to tell herself. But the reward of an evening with him was just too much to give up. After all, it wasn't as if anything was going to happen. They were merely two friends going out to enjoy themselves.

She couldn't help taking extra care when dressing and put on fresh make-up. She twisted her long hair into a knot on top and secured it with a coppery clip. Not bad, she decided, looking at the finished effect.

'You look nice, dear,' Sally told her when Fliss went into the kitchen. 'You going out somewhere?'

'Matt's taking me to hear a band,' she said as casually as she could.

'That's nice,' Sally said abstractedly. 'I don't know what's the matter with this damned mixer. Why does every-thing always have to go wrong at the same time?' she grumbled.

Fliss went to look. It was quite dead. She looked at the cable.

'Good grief,' she shouted. 'Don't touch

it. The cable's completely severed, half-way down. It's a wonder you didn't get a shock, Mum.'

She switched it off at the wall socket and then reached for the fuse box and pulled out the fuse. After examining the mixer lead, she saw that she could fix it, albeit with a shorter cable.

'It's amazing that it could have gone like that. In fact, I don't believe it could have by accident. It looks to me as if it's been deliberately cut through. But who in their right mind would do something like that? The whole place could have burned down, given time.

'Oh, Fliss. Everything's going wrong, isn't it?'

'Certainly we've had a run of bad luck recently. But nothing that has defeated us, has it?'

As soon as dinner was over, Fliss went to get her coat and found Matt waiting near the reception desk.

'You don't mind driving, do you?' he asked her.

'Oh, no, of course not.'

'Only I don't have a car with me.'

'Oh, yes. I noticed it had gone from the car park, come to think of it.'

'But I never did have a car here. I came down by train and then took a taxi from the station.'

'I thought that people-carrier thing was yours. Must have been someone walking who left it there. And here I was, thinking you were going out rather a lot. One should never assume things about people, should one?'

'Certainly not. And while we're on the subject . . . '

'So, it's the drive of a lifetime for you in The Pot, is it?' she interrupted.

'What is The Pot, for heaven's sake?'

'My little car, Pot the Peugeot. Look at the number plate. P-O-T, see?'

'Very original. Let's go then. Do I need any protective clothing? Hard hat, for instance?'

'Any more comments like that and you're walking,' she replied with a grin. 'So why no car?'

'I usually live in London and it just

isn't necessary. In fact it's a liability. Parking is a nightmare and there are traffic jams everywhere. Besides, the transport system is fine, once you get it sussed.'

'Try living without a car in parts of Cornwall and you could go mad. The last buses to most places barely give you time even to have a meal out. It's fine as long as you don't have a business to run or want to go to any evening entertainment.'

'You have a point, but I must say, I haven't really felt that I wanted to do much since I've been here. It's very peaceful. Something seems to take you over in a place like this.'

'Lucky old you.'

Half an hour later, they drove round Truro looking for a parking spot.

'Think I may try parking at the radio station after all. Never many people there at night.'

The pub, when they got there, was noisy and crowded. The music was exciting and the atmosphere everything they wanted. Conversation was impossible so they gave themselves up to the music. Because she was driving, Fliss didn't drink anything alcoholic. Matt settled for beer and seemed perfectly at ease with the surroundings.

'Thanks, that was really good,' he said as they went back to the car. 'Great fun. Haven't enjoyed a band like that for years. Quite takes me back to my university days.'

'Are you suggesting it was a good, old-fashioned evening?'

' 'Course not. Just the feel of it all. I've been allowing myself to sink into a premature middle-aged attitude,' he said with a laugh.

'How old are you?' she asked before she could stop herself.

'Wrong side of thirty. How about you?'

'Twenty-five. Maybe I admit to being the wrong side of twenty-five.'

'A mere child.'

She hit him with her elbow.

As they pulled up in the hotel car

park, Fliss was relieved to see that the lights were all blazing out of the windows.

'At least the power's still on,' she remarked. 'I wonder what new disasters have happened while we've been away.'

She told him about the mixer cable and some of the other problems of the past few days.

'Keep a note of everything, Fliss. Write it somewhere with exact details of time when discovered and cost, if any, of repairs. It may be important if someone really is trying to damage the business.'

'But s'pose it is Mum who's at fault? She does seem to get muddled more easily.'

'It's only natural. If you think it even possible that you have left things on or damaged something, you naturally don't remember causing it. It builds up inside and then as things continue to go wrong, you assume it really must be your fault.'

'I suppose so. But it's only been

happening since I started my job. Does seem a bit of a coincidence.'

'It simply means there are more chances of finding the place empty.'

'Maybe you're right.'

They got out of the car and listened to the pounding of the waves on the shingle. The wind had dropped considerably and the moon shone through the clouds.

'Lovely sea smell,' Fliss remarked. 'Slightly salt, slightly seaweedy.'

'I know what you mean,' Matt said softly.

He was about to reach out for Fliss's arm when she dived off suddenly.

'Good grief. Whatever is that?' she called as she crossed the car park.

There was a cardboard box which was moving slightly, a muffled sound coming from it. Matt joined her. He reached down and pulled the top open.

'Whatever it is, it's firmly stuck down with tape. Good heavens. There's an animal inside.'

'What sort of animal?' she asked in trepidation.

'One that miaows. Could be a kitten.'

'We'd better take it inside and have a look. We can't leave it outside. Who on earth would do such a thing?'

'Someone who didn't want it and had no thoughts for the cruelty of a living creature. I'd slice them in two if I caught them,' he said vehemently.

Carefully, he carried the box into the hotel. Fliss picked up scissors from behind the desk and carefully slit along the taped top. The miaows grew more insistent and gently, she lifted the lid. Two tiny tabby kittens sat peering out startled by the bright lights after confinement in their prison.

'Two of them. Oh, how sweet,' she said softly, reaching in.

The kittens hissed and one stuck its claws into her hand.

'Ouch, ungrateful, little creature.'

'You can't blame them. The human race hasn't done much for them so far. They're probably hungry, thirsty and scared half out of their wits.'

'I'll get them some milk and see what's lying around to feed them. All cats like to eat fish, don't they?'

'Once they're weaned. These two are pretty small. I'd just go for the milk for now. We can experiment later with proper food.'

Fliss poured out two saucers of milk and put them on the floor. Matt lifted the box down to the floor and they waited till the kittens plucked up enough courage to leave their shelter. They homed in on the milk and began to lap greedily.

'Poor things are half starved. I'll get them some more,' Fliss said.

'Leave it at that for now. They'll need some more later. Don't want to make them ill.'

'You're quite the expert, aren't you?'

'Not really, but I did have a cat when I was a kid. Don't tell me you didn't,' Matt added.

'We always lived in the hotel. They're often more trouble than it's worth, keeping them out of the kitchen and everything. I'd better take them up to my room for tonight. Then I can feed them if they need it. So much for my ever catching up on sleep.'

'Thanks for the evening. I really enjoyed it. We should do it again sometime.'

Fliss locked the main door and turned off the lights. She picked up the box and the kittens, now warm and happy after their drink, and went up to her room. She thought abut the evening and her growing relationship with Matt. They seemed to share many interests and enjoy the same sort of things. He also had a very gentle side to him. His treatment and concern over the two kittens had surprised her. He was surprisingly gentle for so large a man. The sight of the tiny kitten sitting in his hand had made her smile fondly. It had looked very secure and relaxed. Dreamily, she imagined being held by him. She gave herself a small shake. This was yet another night when she was allowing her imagination to run riot.

'He is simply not available,' she told herself. 'Forget it.'

But however hard she tried, it was not so easy. Handsome men like Matt Forbes did not appear too often. Handsome, gentle and thoroughly nice men like Matt Forbes were even more of a rarity.

6

Fliss, wake up,' Sally called the next morning, tapping on the door and going in. 'Goodness, whatever have you been doing in here?'

Fliss sat up blinking. The two kittens were curled up on her discarded clothes from the night before and the box was tipped over.

' 'Morning, Mum. These two little characters were dumped in the car park last night. They'd both be dead if I hadn't found them. It was freezing out there. Can you believe anyone would do such a thing?'

'Aren't they sweet? But you can't mean to keep them, not here, in your room.'

'Haven't thought about it much.'

'At least I know where the milk went last night. I thought it was another of my memory losses. I knew I'd left two pints in the fridge and now there's only one.'

'Sorry. Does that make you short for breakfast?'

'I'll manage. I'll do fruit and yogurt, instead of cereal today. I used a lot more than I intended yesterday but the milkman won't be long. Shall I take your little tigers downstairs for you?'

'Little tigers. Good name.'

She rubbed her hand where she'd been scratched the night before.

'Tiger One and Tiger Two. Don't worry, I'll phone the RSPCA later.'

'See you do,' Sally called. 'Can't do with anything else ripping the place apart.'

Fliss looked around her room. She must find some way of leaving them safe for the day. She couldn't risk leaving them outside in the cold and her mother had enough to do with all the hotel work. Maybe the bathroom would be the best place. At least the floor was tiled and any mishaps could be easily cleaned. There wasn't too much to damage available to them.

'They're the most appealing, little creatures,' Sally admitted before Fliss left for work. 'But I'm not sure I can cope with them on my own, not with everything else.'

She told her mother her temporary plan and again promised to phone the RSPCA. She left for work in her usual hurry.

'Enjoy the band, did you?' Rick asked her later that day.

'I did as it happens. Why, were you there?' she replied. 'I didn't see you at all.'

'I didn't think you had. You were rather engrossed in your companion. So, Mummy managed alone last night, did she?'

'What do you mean?'

'It's all right, Fliss. You didn't need to make excuses to turn me down. I simply didn't realise you had a boyfriend.'

'But I haven't. I wasn't making excuses. Matt's just a friend. He's a long-term guest at the hotel. I was showing him some of the local night life.'

'I see. Well, I won't bother you again. He looked pretty much like a boyfriend to me. But who am I to judge? No offence and just ask if you ever fancy a change of companion. The apron strings are slightly longer than I'd realised.'

'Don't be sarcastic, Rick. I really do have to help Mum. It isn't a case of being tied to anybody's apron strings. Things are very tough at present and we're doing our best to make a go of things. If we don't succeed, we might have to sell the place. I don't think either of us could bear that.'

'Sorry, Fliss. I was being thoughtless. And seriously, if you do ever fancy a night out, I'd be happy to take you somewhere, meal, cinema, band or just for a drink, unless that guy who isn't really your boyfriend, objects.'

'Thanks, Rick. That's nice of you. Maybe we could do something once the current crisis is over.'

He smiled and nodded and went back to his work, whistling tunelessly as he did so.

By the time she got home that evening, the kittens had won everyone's hearts. She realised with a stab of shame that she had done nothing at all about finding them a permanent home. The two lady guests and her mother were playing with them in the lounge. There was an assortment of bits of wool and pom-poms to amuse them and it was quite obvious that the three women had spent much of the afternoon with the tiny creatures.

'They're intelligent little things, you know,' Elaine said. 'Very quick to learn.'

'And so cute, aren't you, darling?' Wyn added.

'I'm glad they're such a hit, but don't get too attached. They're not staying, are they, Mum?'

'We-ell,' Sally replied. 'They haven't been much trouble today. When the weather gets better, they could probably be outside most of the time. They'd soon get used to the visitors. What did the RSPCA say?'

'As it happens, I quite forgot to

phone them. It's been another hectic day. And actually, Mum, I have to go out again this evening. I've been asked if I'd be willing to do a recording. Staff shortages and they didn't want to break a promise. They'd agreed to attend some important local event. Nothing much really, but I can't let any chances slip, can I? It's important to me to make a go of this job.'

'Oh, Fliss, two nights running? That's so disappointing. I was hoping you could take a bit of the weight off me and do some orders for me.'

'Can't it wait? I can always do the orders tomorrow.'

Wyn and Elaine were listening with great interest. Fliss was surprised.

'I suppose so but things are slipping back, after all the problems of the last few days. It hasn't been easy, you know, dear.'

'It must take such a lot of time to run this place single-handed. I'm surprised you manage to keep up the struggle,' Wyn said.

'It's only been any sort of problem since I've been going out to work as well,' Fliss protested. 'It's only temporary.'

'Then you are to be commended for showing such diligence to a temporary position,' Wyn said. 'Not many girls today would be so willing.'

'I suppose you like the power of being in charge of the broadcast to the whole country,' Elaine added.

'Not exactly, but it was fun when I stood in the other day. I'm only the receptionist really, but Cornwall Radio is a small company and they do specialise in giving local talent a chance. Anyhow, Mum, if there's anything you want me to do, I have an hour spare before I need to go.'

'You'd better put these two somewhere safe. I'll get on with dinner now.'

'And what delights are on the menu tonight?' Wyn asked.

'I've got some nice plaice. Thought I'd simply grill it and serve with a butter and lemon sauce.'

'I do find too much fish gives me

indigestion,' Elaine murmured.

'Indigestion?' Fliss echoed. 'I thought fish was the one thing that was always fed to invalids because it's so easily digested.'

'I'm hardly an invalid, dear. No, I simply don't care for too much fish.'

'Perhaps you'd like something else,' Sally offered. 'A nice omelette or gammon, perhaps?'

'An omelette sounds nice. And what might you put into it?'

'What would you like?'

'Prawns might be tasty,' Elaine said delicately.

'Aren't they perhaps a little too fishy?' Fliss retorted.

The two women glared.

'I think it's time we went up to dress,' Wyn said hastily.

Sally shook her head at her daughter as they left, afraid that she may say something else to irritate the guests.

'Really, Fliss. You've no need to upset them. We really need their booking.'

'Sorry, Mum, but you must admit,

they do twitter on a bit. Poor Matt doesn't feel safe left in the same room as them.'

'Don't exaggerate, but, Fliss, I genuinely do need your help, you know. I can't manage everything. I don't know. Just recently, with so much going wrong, I wonder if it is worth all the effort.'

'Oh, Mum, I'm sorry. I wasn't thinking. I must do this interview though. I promised. I adore these little tigers already, but I accept what you say. A hotel is no place for keeping them.'

She took them upstairs. Matt came out of his room as she was passing.

'Hi, there,' he said with one of his devastating smiles. 'The kittens, I presume?' he asked, nodding towards the box she carried.

'Yes. Getting them out of the way while Mum's cooking.'

'I take it the RSPCA didn't want to know.'

'I never got round to phoning. I can't

see any alternative though. I'm not here most of the time and until they've grown, I can hardly put them outside. I'm locking them safely in my bathroom for the evening.'

'Sounds as if you plan to go somewhere.'

'Yes. I've got a recording to do for the radio. Should be fun.'

'Good for you. Enjoy yourself.'

He went back into his room and shut the door. She stood for a second longer, her thoughts racing. She wanted so much to be more than casual friends, but it could not be. She took a deep breath and continued along to her own room.

As she got herself ready, the kittens ran around the floor. She smiled at their antics. They patted one of the pom-poms and engaged in mock fights. How could anyone have simply dumped them like that? Such people should never be allowed to keep animals again. She changed her clothes and shut the kittens firmly into her bathroom. They couldn't do any damage there, she thought. She went down again, to help her mother in the little time she had left.

'I'd better get you something to eat, before you go,' Sally said, looking very flustered.

'Don't worry. I can get a sandwich or something when I get back. I shouldn't be long, once I find the place, that is. Look, Mum, if it really is too much for you, we can get some help in. There's sure to be a school girl in the village wanting a bit of part-time work. I have to keep on with this job while it lasts. We need my money, and maybe we could get some more long-stay folks. Christmas is only a month away. We can really pull the stops out and make it a Christmas to remember.'

'And give ourselves even more to do. I see. And where does your precious job fit into all of this?'

'I have to go, Mum. It isn't like you to be so negative. I won't be late. We can talk when I get back.'

She reached into the fridge and pulled out a piece of cheese.

'That'll keep the wolves at bay for now,' she joked.

All the same, she frowned as soon as she was out of her mother's sight. Never before had Sally complained about having too much to do. It was very worrying.

The interview was fun. It was recorded for broadcast later in the week and covered the opening of a new centre for youngsters in the centre of town. The idea was to provide a venue similar to a club but designed especially for teenagers who were too young to drink. On sale was a variety of soft drinks, at reasonable prices. There was a good sound system and the chance for local groups to play and entertain. Everyone was very excited about it and this was the opening night party.

Fliss got some excellent comments from the organisers and new members and even taped some of the music. It was ten o'clock before she left and she suddenly realised she was absolutely starving. She couldn't allow her mother to cook anything when she got home, so she stopped at a takeaway and bought a kebab. She sat in the car and munched the hot savoury. It felt very strange to be eating like this after the strictures of the hotel but her meal tasted wonderful. She screwed up the paper and set off for home. Again, she noted the lights with some relief. Since the storm, she felt unnerved, uncertain. She felt less relieved when she got into the reception.

Matt was standing in a way that could only be interpreted as aggressively.

'Those dratted kittens have no place in the hotel. Untrained, little savages. They've all but totally ruined my laptop. All the work I've done for the past week is now lost. Explain that to my publishers.'

'What's going on?' Fliss demanded.

'Your blasted cats. That's what.'

'But they're safely locked in my bathroom. Aren't they?'

She looked at her mother.

'I'm afraid not, dear,' Wyn, who had also appeared, said coldly. 'They've run amok for the entire evening. Quite shredded several of my more expensive garments and ruined poor Mr Forbes's computer machine. And they've been into Elaine's room as well. She's so distraught, I've had to come down for a brandy for her.'

Sally reached for the ordinary bottle and poured some of the golden liquid into a glass.

'Thank you, dear. Most kind. But I was going to have one myself, too. Can't expect it free.'

'Of course you must. Have doubles,' Fliss said angrily. 'I really can't think how the kittens got out. I know I locked them in very firmly and they can't reach a five-foot-high door knob.'

'You may have thought you did. But the proof is there.'

'Your brandy,' Sally interrupted hastily, as she recognised the signs of Fliss's temper fraying.

'Thank you,' Wyn said stiffly, and, accepting the drinks, she turned and went upstairs.

'Matt, do you want one?' Sally asked.

'No, thanks. I'd like to know how soon your insurance is going to cough up for a new laptop. Cat's urine doesn't exactly improve anything electronic.'

'Matt, I'm so dreadfully sorry, but I did lock them in, truly. I'll organise a new machine for you right away. We won't wait for the insurance. Anyhow, I don't think they'll cover pet damage. We didn't have any pets when we took out the new policy.'

'And we won't have them for much longer,' Sally assured him.

'I thought you liked the kittens,' Fliss said wearily. 'Where are they now, by the way?'

'In the shed,' Sally replied. 'Only safe place to leave them.'

'Poor little things,' Fliss said with unaccustomed tears pressing hard behind her eyes. 'Not much of a life so far. Dumped by one lot of owners and abandoned by the next. And whatever anyone says or thinks, I did leave them safely locked in.'

'Perhaps now you know how I felt when you thought I'd left the soup pan on, and the door unlocked, the freezer turned off and all the other stupid things that have been going wrong. Don't deny that's what you were thinking. I've seen the looks on your faces. Poor old thing's going batty. Have to make allowances.'

'I think everyone's getting rather over-wrought,' Matt interrupted gently. 'I'm sorry I blew my top but you can understand why, I'm sure.'

'Didn't you keep a copy of your book?' Fliss enquired.

'Not for the last couple of days. I know. Don't say it. That is indeed a seriously bad mistake. But then, I don't always keep a copy. Perhaps the machine can be rescued. I assumed that it was more than water that had been spilled on it. Let's sleep on it. Maybe things will look better in the morning.'

'That's very understanding of you,' Sally told him.

'Goodnight then.'

Matt crossed to the stairs and disappeared from their sight.

'I'm sure someone is causing all the damage and chaos,' Fliss said thoughtfully. 'I mean to say, everything is very petty on the surface but causes a lot of upset and confusion, not to mention the cost. If that mixer had caught fire, for instance, just think of the possible damage. It could so easily have killed someone, too. I'm certain someone's got it in for us, Mum.'

'What can we do about it?'

'We could tell the police.'

'What good would that do? The police would need proof, evidence that we weren't making it up for some strange reason. But who on earth could be doing it? And why?'

'Matt was probably the only person who knew where I was going to leave the kittens. Perhaps he let them out.'

'You're not serious. Why on earth

would he want to do that? Besides, it was his property that was damaged.'

'Suppose something was already wrong? The machine didn't work properly or his book wasn't going as well as it should. This would give him a perfect excuse.'

'I think it's time you were in bed. We'll deal with the wretched kittens tomorrow.'

Fliss lay awake for ages, thinking over the past few weeks. Both she and her mother had been totally stressed to begin with. Trying to manage a job and help organise the running of the hotel was proving difficult. The problems were only destined to get more complicated, especially if she did decide to pursue her career in local radio. She'd been very lucky so far and she had thoroughly enjoyed the very different challenges.

If they did decide to sell the hotel, she could maybe have a completely new start and her mum could retire and probably be financially comfortable for the rest of her life. On the other hand, Sally was simply too young to retire and had been used to running her own business for many years. Moving away from the hotel would cause her great distress. Sally had lived here since she had been married and Fliss had been here all her life.

With a heavy heart, the next morning, Fliss called the animal charity. She explained the situation and the officer promised to get over to collect the kittens as soon as he could.

'They're like two miniature tigers,' she said miserably. 'Very cute and typically naughty, little kittens.'

'Then we should have no difficulty in finding homes for them, should we, madam?'

'I s'pose not. But you will try to keep them together, won't you?'

'We'll try but no promises. Not everyone can cope with two kittens, can they, ma'am?'

'But they're so little. And they've had a really tough call from life so far.'

'Do you want us to collect them or not, miss?'

'I don't at all, but my mother can't cope with them. Not with the business, too, and I'm out at work. So we don't have much choice, do we?'

'Sounds as if you don't. Leave it to us. We'll do what we can. See you later.'

'I'll go and give them a last drink of milk,' Fliss said to her mother.

'The condemned cats' last meal,' Sally announced in dramatic tones. 'For heaven's sake, Fliss, snap out of it. They were abandoned in our car park. We've done what we can for them. Now it's up to someone else.'

'Of course, you're right. You usually are. I'd better go now. Good luck.'

She went out and spent the next minutes saying her goodbyes. The kittens miaowed pitifully and briefly. She considered taking them to work with her. It was a futile thought.

'Goodbye, little tigers,' she whispered and left quickly.

7

I had to get a new laptop in the end,' Matt told her, almost as soon as she walked in that evening. 'I took the old one in and they said it was beyond repair. Gave me a reasonable deal and even thought they might be able to retrieve my book from the old machine. No promises yet, of course.'

'We'll pay for the computer,' Fliss promised. 'I'm afraid we can't manage it all at once, but I will pay you something each week.'

'There's no need. I was angry at the time. It was getting old anyhow. Let's say the kittens clinched the deal.'

'I insist,' Fliss told him. 'You mustn't be out of pocket through no fault of your own.'

'We'll argue about it later. I take the young offenders have now left?'

'I guess so. They were here for such a

short time but I really miss them.'

'How about another trip out this evening? See if we can find some more musical entertainment.'

'OK. Maybe not tonight though. I don't think I ought to leave Mum. She wants me to help with some ordering and stuff. Tomorrow?'

'Fine by me. Look, Fliss, I'm really sorry about the things I said last night. I was angry and upset.'

He put his hand on her arm as he spoke. It felt like fire striking her and she flinched slightly.

'Sorry? Is something wrong?' he asked.

'No, of course not. Sorry. You er . . . er . . . you made me jump.'

How could she tell him that his touch seemed like an electric shock hitting her? She couldn't say anything because it sounded too ridiculous. Besides, it obviously meant nothing to him. Then he gripped her arm even more tightly.

If he tries to kiss me, I won't be able to say no. I just know I won't, raced through her mind.

'There's something I wanted to ask you.'

'OK. Ask away,' she said, feeling her heart pounding away, extra loudly.

'Would it be OK for me to have a guest stay for the weekend after next? I didn't think you'd mind, as you're not full.'

' 'Course we don't mind. We shall be delighted,' she replied, still feeling as if her heart was trying to bang its way out of her chest. 'Anyone special?' she asked, a sudden fear gripping her as she realised it must be his wife.

'Oh, pretty special. I meant to ask Sally earlier but I wasn't sure which weekend would be suitable. I've now spoken to my guest and that's the best weekend. Will you tell Sally or do you want me to tell her?'

'I'll put it in the book.'

'Oh, I caught your interview on local radio today, by the way. It was good, very good. You've got a nice voice for radio. Comes over really well.'

She went pink with pleasure.

'Thanks a lot,' she replied. 'I really enjoy it.'

'If you do ever sell the hotel, it looks as though you could find an opening in radio, maybe.'

'We don't plan to sell up, thank you very much. Now, if there's nothing else, I shall go and curl up with a book for half an hour. As a writer, you must approve of that.'

'Now that depends on what you're reading.'

'Oh, only some light, romantic nonsense. I use it to unwind.'

'That's just how it should be. Whom do you like? I'm interested in people's tastes.'

'I like several authors.'

She named a few well-known ones.

'I know it isn't considered worthwhile reading but I like it better than some of the so-called more literary, modern people. Most of it I find quite unreadable. I do like Mae Morris's stuff, though. She shows a very clear understanding of how women's minds work. Relationships are so important, aren't they? She often says exactly what I think about things. Stupid really, I s'pose. Real life is never like the books suggest.'

'Don't be so defensive, Fliss. As it happens, I think it's just the right sort of thing to unwind with. You're hardly likely to sit down with something like War and Peace to relax every day. It's much too heavy to hold, for one thing. Tends to fall in the bath, too.'

Fliss laughed. She had read many worthy books in her time but just now, she could only concentrate on something easy and light.

'So, you like to read in the bath, do you? Such luxury to soak in a bath. I've never time for more than a quick shower myself!'

He smiled gently, and said, 'I'll see you later perhaps. Have confidence in yourself. Have confidence in what you enjoy doing, reading in particular. People make me cross when they apologise for reading romance. It would upset romantic fiction writers if everyone apologised for reading their work.'

'I s'pose you're right. See you later.'

She went up to her room and lay down on the bed. She read a few words before falling into an uneasy doze. When she awoke, she couldn't remember quite why she felt so depressed. Then she remembered. Matt had a guest coming to stay. Who else could it be but his wife? That was going to be extra tough, watching them together and knowing they shared so much.

She did admit to a certain curiosity, however. She was curious to know the sort of woman he would choose. Jealous? Of course she wasn't jealous. She'd have to decide if she mentioned the fact that she and Matt had been out together, shared meals together and often talked for several hours. It was up to Matt really. He hadn't told her to keep it quiet.

Wait and see what she's like, she told herself firmly.

And foolish notions of romance between them were simply figments of her own imagination. How could any man like him still be unmarried or unattached in any way? He was surely every woman's dream man. He couldn't possibly have reached the wrong side of thirty, as he put it, and still be available.

'Matt has a guest coming next weekend. I think it must be his wife,' Fliss told her mother later.

'Really? I didn't think he had one. He's never mentioned her to me.'

'Oh, he has to me.'

Fliss thought about her words. Had he really talked about her? Every time he tried to bring up the subject, she always turned him away from it. She didn't want to hear.

'I assume then, they'll be sharing a room?' Sally asked.

'I suppose so. I forgot to ask. You can sort that out, can't you? Now, shall we get down to this ordering, and any other things we need to talk about? I'm going to be out tomorrow evening, so I'd like to get it done tonight.'

'Again? Going somewhere nice?'

'Just to another pub concert.'

'What, with Matt?'

'Yes. Why not?'

'Well, is it right? If he really does have a wife, I mean?'

'Orders, Mum. Let's get on with them.'

*   *   *

'It isn't Matt's wife coming to stay,' Sally announced in triumph. 'In fact what he told me led me to believe he doesn't have one. It's a teenage boy who's coming. Jason Forbes.'

'I see. His son then. Wonder where he lives the rest of the time? Boarding school, I expect.'

Matt was rather ill-at-ease as the visit of Jason Forbes drew closer. When he finally arrived, Fliss could see why. The boy, a younger, immature version of Matt, looked thoroughly bored from the moment he arrived. The weather was very cold that day and it was inclined to rain every few minutes. They played a listless game of chess and then Jason went to his room to watch TV.

'Would you consider coming to a concert with us tonight?' Matt asked Fliss when they were alone.

'What, me, with you and Jason? Is that really a good idea?'

' 'Course it is. Why wouldn't it be?'

'Well, it's been some time since you saw Jason so perhaps you should spend the time exclusively with him.'

'He'll be delighted to have someone else there. Believe me.'

'OK. What's on?'

'Some group that's in the charts, non-stop. I want to prove to Jason that Cornwall isn't completely devoid of life. He'd probably have liked the group we saw in the pub last week but he's too young to go into pubs.'

'I didn't realise you were into that sort of stuff,' Fliss said with a grin.

'I'm not, but I hope he is. I couldn't

face another evening of glowering across the dinner table. Would your mum mind if we have an early dinner? You could join us if you've got the time.'

'I'm sure she wouldn't mind. But I think I might decline to join you. I'll grab something on the hoof.'

'Horse steaks you mean? Didn't know you got them here.'

'Fool!'

She laughed, punching his arm gently. He caught her hand and held it. The feeling of electricity surging between them made her catch her breath. It had happened again. She felt herself blushing and tried to pull away.

'Why do you always try to resist me? Any time I have tried to draw close, you pull away. I'm sorry. I thought you liked me.'

'I do, Matt, very much. But it wouldn't be right, would it?'

'I don't see why not.'

'Perhaps I'm just an old-fashioned girl with principles.'

'Surely that doesn't extend to a small kiss? A harmless kiss?'

'Maybe I'm scared. I'm not sure I could stop anything it might lead to.'

'Now that does sound promising.'

'Please, Matt. Anyone could come in. Jason for instance.'

'What's he got to do with it?'

'You should ask him. He's just come down the stairs.'

That evening was not a great success. Unfortunately, it seemed that the band appearing was last month's hit and so was now totally out of fashion. Evidently the tour was ending at this particular venue and that made it even more apparent that Cornwall was indeed the end of the world, as far as Jason was concerned.

'I can't believe you want to live in this god-forsaken place,' he muttered angrily during the interval.

'You're simply not seeing Cornwall at its best,' Matt told him. 'Don't be so quick to judge.'

'So, does this suggest that you are

thinking of moving down here permanently?' Fliss ventured.

'I'd hoped to find some suitable property. Not much around though, at present.'

'Not a good time of the year for Cornwall. Loads of people take their property off the market and wait for spring. And how do you feel about the idea of Cornwall, Jason?' she asked.

'Dunno. Don't suppose what I think matters. Matt always does what he wants anyhow.'

'I'm sorry, I have to go to the gents,' Matt announced.

Obviously troubled at leaving them alone, he was tentative. He hesitated and looked from one to the other.

'We'll manage without you for a moment,' Fliss reassured him.

She was delighted to have the brief chance to pump Jason for information. Probably exactly what Matt was dreading, she thought.

'So,' she began, 'what do you do with yourself most of the time?'

'School,' he replied without any enthusiasm.

'Boarding school?'

'Yep. Not much choice with Matt always on the move.'

'And what about your mother?'

The boy stared at her in surprise.

'Should have thought Matt would have told you. She's dead. Car accident, a long time ago.'

'Oh, I am sorry,' Fliss stammered. 'I'd no idea.'

No wonder Matt was so reticent about her, and the fact he didn't drive a car could have something to do with it. Within a few seconds, she had written the whole scenario. A few concrete facts and she had the story mapped out. It also meant that Matt was free after all, she realised with delight. He may have a son and be a widower but at least he wasn't married. She felt herself smiling and as the man in question returned to his seat, she gave him a broad grin.

'Missed me?' he asked jokingly.

'Good chance to sort out my brain,'

she replied enigmatically.

The next time he touched her or tried to kiss her, she knew she could respond with a clear conscience.

'How about a pizza on the way home?' she suggested.

'Reckon I could manage that,' Jason said, cheering up a little.

Over the meal, Fliss unashamedly pumped Matt about his plans for a permanent move down to Cornwall.

'Well, I do have my eye on one particular place that might soon be on the market. I've heard a few rumours.'

A nasty thought insinuated itself into Fliss's mind. While on the surface, she was chatting happily to Matt and his son, she kept thinking of the particular place he might have been talking about. She suddenly decided with blinding clarity and stopped, her fork poised halfway to her mouth. He wanted Penmore Point Hotel! That was his plan. He would never run it as a hotel but he intended to turn it into a private residence. And what a residence it would make, perfect location, plenty of space.

'I see,' she mumbled.

'It's actually in the next village to you. What's the matter? You look odd,' he went on.

'I'm sorry. It's my brain being hyperactive. Always jumping to conclusions. Bit like your wife, I suppose.'

'Your wife?' Jason echoed. 'You're not married, are you?'

''Course not,' Matt replied, highly amused at the thought.

'Jason told me what you have been hedging around all these weeks. I'm so sorry, Matt. I didn't realise your wife was dead.'

Jason sat grinning. This was getting interesting.

'So, you did have a wife? You never even invited me to the wedding. Rotter,' he teased.

'Hang on a minute. Exactly who do you think Jason is?' Matt asked.

'Your son.'

At this point, Jason broke into

guffaws of laughter.

'Think I'd have a dork like him for a dad? You gotta be joking. He's my brother, aren't you, bad man?'

' 'Fraid so. I'd have been a bit precocious to have a son of his age. He's fourteen and I'm only thirty-one.'

'You'd have been seventeen,' Jason challenged him. 'Certainly possible.'

'In the middle of 'A'-levels and planning on going to university? I don't think so, my boy.'

'I always suspected there was something odd about us two,' Jason said mysteriously. 'You never treated me like a brother should.'

'What are you blathering about? We're seventeen years apart, for heaven's sake. I was off to university practically before you could sit up.'

'So you say, bad man,' Jason said with a wicked grin. 'So, maybe you didn't marry her.'

'This is ridiculous and you know it. I haven't got nor ever have had a wife. And what is more . . . '

'But you told me you had,' Fliss interrupted.

'When did I tell you that?'

'When I asked you. You said you didn't want to talk about her, almost the first time you spoke to me.'

'I don't even remember.'

He paused and something obviously clicked in his memory.

'Oh, Fliss. You are such an incredible leaper to conclusions. I remember I said I didn't want to talk about a wife. It was only because I don't have a wife, of any sort. What sort of bloke do you take me for? I'd hardly be asking an eligible female to go out with me if all the time I were married, now, would I?'

'I suppose not. But how was I to know?'

'I think it's time we left,' Matt said suddenly, seeming angry.

'I'm sorry, Matt,' she apologised.

'OK. It's very hurtful that you could think that of me. You must admit it.'

In silence, Fliss drove them back to the hotel. There was a chill between them that seemed to be growing even colder. She must learn to curb her tongue and somehow learn to stop taking a few facts and jumping to the sort of conclusions she usually did from them.

'Thanks for the lift,' Matt said shortly.

'Yep, thanks,' Jason said after a sharp nudge from his brother.

'Thank you for the concert and the pizza,' Fliss replied politely.

She cursed under her breath. Now she knew for certain that Matt was unattached, she'd completely blown it. She bit her lip, wondering how earth she could begin to apologise.

'Good-night, Fliss. I'm sorry you have such a low opinion of me. I really liked you.'

Matt then went inside, a disgruntled Jason trailing behind him.

Fliss stared after them, locking the car carefully. She felt totally deflated and an utter dimwit.

8

There was a degree of tension in the air the following morning. The two lady guests seemed to find fault with a number of petty things. They complained the milk wasn't hot enough for their coffee and their toast was slightly too well done. Fliss was in charge of the breakfasts as it was Sunday and she wanted to give her mum a bit of a rest. She didn't believe for a moment that the complaints were justified. All the same, she did her best to put things right without allowing her irritation to show.

When Matt and Jason came down for breakfast, they looked as if they had been having words. They both seemed a little short-tempered, especially, she thought, towards her. For once, she didn't retaliate and removed their plates silently. She would be glad when today was over.

'It's terribly cold out today, isn't it?' Elaine said to Matt, obviously hoping to begin a conversation.

'Haven't been out yet,' Matt replied, almost politely.

'And what do you and your son have planned for today?' she continued.

Fliss couldn't help but stay to listen. She was quite curious herself about their plans.

'I don't wish to be rude, Miss Derricoat, but he is not my son. Secondly, I really don't think it's any of your business what we plan to do.'

'Really,' she protested. 'You don't have to be quite so rude. I think we'll go out today, after all, Wyn. There's an unpleasant atmosphere about the place today. Don't you agree?'

'Oh, yes. Someone, or some people even, must have got out of bed on the wrong side.'

She cast a glance in Fliss's direction and then looked back at Matt and Jason. She turned back to her friend and spoke in a loud stage whisper.

'If he isn't his son, who do you think he can be?'

Fliss went into the kitchen, muttering softly, 'Nosey, old women.'

She saw that Sally had left a large lamb joint sitting on the side defrosting. She cursed. She was supposed to ask if any of them wanted a Sunday roast lunch. She gritted her teeth and went back into the dining room to ask the guests.

'We were planning to stay in,' Wyn replied. 'But in view of the atmosphere here, we've changed our minds.'

'Fine,' Fliss replied, not allowing her feelings to show in any way.

She turned to Matt and Jason and asked them.

'We'll probably go out for a long walk. What do you want to do, Jason?'

'Sunday dinner sounds good. I'll have missed school evening meal by the time I get back.'

'OK. We'll be in for lunch. Thank you.'

Matt spoke the words quite without

warmth. Fliss felt alternately sad and angry. Obviously, his morals were not as obvious as he thought. Granted, she acknowledged, it was her arriving at the wrong conclusion that had started the whole thing but she had said she was sorry, hadn't she?

'Right,' she said in clipped tones. 'What time would suit you?'

'Better make it twelve-thirty to make sure we get to the station in time for Jason's train.'

She nodded in agreement and went back to the kitchen. She noticed the puddle beneath the fridge just a few moments later. How had she missed it before? Somehow, the plug had been pulled out. First the freezer and now the fridge. This was too much. It was clearly no accident. The plug and socket were right behind the large piece of equipment. This was deliberate sabotage.

She opened the door and sighed. Why hadn't she noticed it when she has taken the milk and eggs out? What was more, the entire contents of the fridge were all mixed up and in the wrong places. There was thawed chicken on the top shelf, sitting next to a cooked ham. Cheese and butter were low down, spots of thawed blood coating their surface. Regrettable though it was, the entire contents would probably have to go.

Both she and her mother were meticulous in the way they stored food and followed the rules about separating cooked and frozen meat. Their food hygiene had always been a priority. Not only had the saboteur caused the food to be too warm, they had obviously known something of the laws covering food hygiene to have mixed things so effectively.

It had to be someone here, in the hotel, but who could want to do such a thing? It had to be Matt. Who else? The two women were far too wimpish to do anything like this. The man himself came to the kitchen door.

'Excuse me, but could we have some

more milk, please? Teenage boys have insatiable appetites for cereal.'

'You want Penmore, don't you?' Fliss flung at him.

'What are you talking about? It would be very nice, but I'm . . . '

'You want to buy Penmore, don't you? You're behind all these accidents, aren't you? You've done a thorough job here. Very clever. You've even mixed things up in the fridge to ensure maximum damage and loss.'

'Felice, just stop that mouth of yours for one minute. No, I'm not behind any of these events. I was going to say that I would love Penmore Point but it is totally out of my reach. I may have a decent amount of capital available but it isn't anywhere near that league. No, I'm looking at a place in the village, a cottage, if you must know. There's enough room for me and Jason and a study for me to write. Very modest, indeed. Forget the milk. We're going out.'

He turned and rushed away, leaving

Fliss very close to tears.

She had just begun to take everything out of the fridge, when she heard the bell on reception ring. Wiping her hands, she went out to the front to see who it was.

'Morning, ma'am. I'd like to speak to the manager, if that's possible,' the stranger said.

'Yes?' Fliss replied. 'I'm joint manager. Well, the hotel is jointly owned by my mother and myself. How may I help?'

'Environmental health inspectorate. I apologise for calling so early on a Sunday but we've had a report of some discrepancies in the way your storage facility is being managed. I need access to the kitchen for an immediate inspection.'

He held out his identification card. She took it and stared at it, not able to read a word.

'What, now?' she gasped. 'But you can't. It isn't convenient. We've had a breakdown overnight. I was just about to clear everything out.'

'I'm sorry. There is no alternative, apart, that is, from closing you down pending a full investigation.'

'Fliss? What's going on?' Sally asked as she appeared behind the inspector, 'Oh, it's Mr Naylor, isn't it? What on earth are you doing here so early on a Sunday?'

'Mrs Crosby, I'm sorry to inconvenience you, but we have to make a spot check on your kitchen. We've received several complaints, I'm afraid.'

'But I don't understand. Of course you can inspect us. We've absolutely nothing to hide.'

'But we have, Mum,' Fliss said warningly. 'Oh, I'd better explain. You have to know sooner or later. Our phantom has been at it again. The big fridge was switched off overnight, and someone has mixed up all the foods. It will all have to be thrown out.'

'Oh, no,' Sally said faintly. 'This is too much. Who reported it?'

'Yes,' Fliss asked, 'tell us that and we may have our saboteur.'

'We don't usually take much notice of anonymous tip-offs but this one sounded so detailed. I'm sorry, I couldn't ignore it. All I know is that it was a man. He withheld his number and gave no name. Now, the fridge, if you please.'

By the time he left, Mr Naylor had discovered eight major and several minor problems. There were food scraps in the sink, vegetable peelings on the floor under the sink and a host of other infringements of the law. They were all things that neither Sally nor Fliss would dream of doing. To top the lot, mouse droppings had been found in one of the storage bins in the cupboard. There had never been any trace of mice in the hotel in all the years they had lived there. It was something they had worked very hard to avoid.

By the time Mr Naylor had finished, they were both thoroughly dejected and very upset. Rather than close them down immediately, the inspector allowed them a week to put things right. He would then return to make another inspection.

'I'm reasonably satisfied with your explanation,' he had told them. 'And there's never been a single problem in the past. If you are really being undermined, perhaps the police should be informed.'

After he left, Fliss made some coffee and sat on a stool next to her mother. Sally spoke softly.

'You know, dear, I really think I've had enough. I can't bear all these dreadful things going wrong constantly. It's more than the inconvenience. We can't afford to lose that much food. After everything we've worked so hard for, this is the end. You've got the start of a career in the radio. Let's sell up and find a nice little cottage some-where. You'll probably get married one of these days, anyhow, and then where would I be?'

'You don't mean it, Mum. We can't allow someone to drive us out of our home.'

'But who can it be?'

144

'As I said before, I still wonder if it could be Matt. Mr Naylor said it was a man's voice on the phone. He denies it of course, Matt, I mean. By the way, did you know he's looking for somewhere to buy locally?'

''Course I know. He's interested in Mrs Trecastle's place. She's thinking of moving up-country to be near her daughter.'

'Oh. No wonder he was annoyed when I accused him of being the saboteur so he could buy Penmore on the cheap.'

'Oh, Fliss,' Sally said reprovingly to her daughter.

'And he isn't married, or a widower,' Fliss went on.

'Oh, you silly girl. Where do you get your ideas from? Really, Fliss. Your brain must be quite addled at times.'

'You're right. I always was good at jumping to conclusions, wasn't I?'

'Is there something else?'

'Jason isn't his son. He's Matt's brother.'

'Yes, dear. He told me.'

Fliss gazed at her mother in disbelief. 'And you let me go on thinking . . . Oh, Mum, why didn't you tell me?'

'Because I assumed you knew. Besides, he isn't old enough to have a son of that age. Anyway, you were happy enough to chat for hours on end and go out with Matt.'

Fliss looked away and blushed very slightly. Sally stared at her daughter and shook her head.

'So, you did all that believing he was a married man? Really, Fliss, I despair of you.'

'I thought everything was all innocent, harmless. I didn't even kiss him. Well, apart from when he kissed me, but that was only a peck on the cheek.'

She touched her cheek as if in memory.

'I guess I'm old-fashioned and I'll never understand you young folk. In my day . . . '

'OK. Don't go on about it. I've ruined everything and I'm a first-class idiot. But now, we really do have to discuss what we are going to do,' Fliss interrupted.

'Throw that lot away for a start,' Sally said, nodding towards the fridge. 'Then we'd better see about lunch. I just hope we can manage with what's in the freezer till I can get to the cash and carry tomorrow.'

Fliss looked away, feeling even more dreadful than she's felt earlier.

They spent a busy morning working to clear up the latest disaster and cooking the lunch. They simply couldn't decide what ought to be done long-term. It seemed that things were moving smoothly enough for the immediate future. After lunch, Fliss offered to drive Jason to the station, to save Matt getting a taxi. He accepted gratefully and Fliss was pleased to have the chance to apologise once more to Matt.

'I suppose I accept your apology, Fliss,' he told her. 'But I'm afraid it has damaged any feelings that were growing towards you. I thought I knew you.'

'But I'm still the same impulsive girl I always was. Tongue runs away with itself.'

'Maybe that's the problem. But I can't reconcile the thought that you could ever believe such bad things about me. Thinking I'd try anything on with you, if I really was a married man. You have a very low opinion of the human race is all I can think.'

'I'm sorry. I've blown it all completely, haven't I?'

'Looks that way. And one more thing,' Matt began, 'if I really wanted to buy your hotel, I'd make a straight offer for it, not try some underhand way to get you turned out of the place.'

'I s'pose you'll want to leave the hotel immediately.'

'No. I have to stay on. I have a deadline to finish my book. I've really fallen behind and my agent is screaming at me for the manuscript. I have let my flat for several months so I literally have nowhere else to go. Perhaps I can stay here and finish. Hopefully, by then, I shall know if I can buy the cottage.'

'So, we may still be almost neighbours,' Fliss said with a hollow laugh. 'You can always be one of our regular customers.'

'Perhaps I can. Who can tell?'

Fliss threw herself into broadcasting work for the next few days. Though it was still weeks from Christmas, there were a number of special recordings taking place. On Christmas Day and Boxing Day themselves, a few people would have to continue the live broadcasts but plenty of pre-recorded programmes lessened the commitments for everyone at the small radio station.

Fliss also managed to do a few more live broadcasts, still finding great pleasure in meeting new people. She discovered that she was able to put people at their ease so they could talk without feeling too nervous. Some of her odd collection of qualifications obviously came in useful, she told herself.

Each evening, then, she tried to help with the work and general organisation of the hotel. She saw little sign of Matt, as he was working very hard to finish his book. She refused to take his meals up to his room, afraid that she might upset him further. She was also scared that she might upset herself. She often found herself thinking about what might have been. Her impetuous nature had ruined everything.

She had made up her mind that she must change, try to be more mature. The trouble was, it took away her sense of fun and she became rather quiet and moody for much of the time she was at home. She even went to a pub concert with Rick one evening, but it was not a great success.

'What's got into you lately?' he asked. 'Finished with lover boy?'

'Lover boy?' she exclaimed. 'We never actually started anything. Like I said before, he's just a guest at our hotel.'

'But you hoped, didn't you?' he said shrewdly. 'I could tell from the way you looked at him, when I saw you that time.'

'I really don't know what you mean,' Fliss protested. 'I never looked at him in any special way.'

'Oh, no?' Rick laughed. 'Oh, it's all right. I'm only teasing you a little. Why don't you simply tell him how you feel? I thought all girls did these days. Go for it. You're not the girl we used to know. Other people have noticed how quiet you've become. Not suitable material for a broadcaster, you know. You could have made something of yourself. Believe me, I hear things. People talk in front of me without noticing I'm there.'

'And I thought if I tried to be more mature, I'd become a more sensible person. I have been working hard to curb my ability to jump to conclusions, usually the wrong ones. Maybe stopping to think isn't exactly the right thing to do for me.'

'Certainly not. Loses spontaneity.'

'Thanks, Rick. You're a good friend.

And I'm sorry if I don't live up to all you hoped.'

'I'm cool. No worries,' he said cheerfully.

For the rest of the evening, she pumped him for information about things he might have overheard about her possible future at Cornwall Radio. She felt gratified by some of the things he told her. The girl on maternity leave, whose job Fliss was covering, had evidently decided not to return. The job could be hers permanently and what was more, there was a chance that she could do more actual broadcasting. Rick had overheard the station manager discussing it with one of the producers. He made her promise not to let on that she knew when the offer was made. Happily, she agreed, though she decided to tell her mother immediately, assuming she didn't count as part of her promise.

The two ladies were hanging on at the hotel, though their interest was obviously flagging. Apart from one or two casual guests, the small community had been together for several weeks now. All the same, Fliss felt closer to them than she ever had and still felt the same sense of irritation with their twittering ways. It was a good job her mother remained so calm and placid. At least she managed to keep the peace.

'Are we going to do anything special for Christmas?' Sally asked one evening in the second week of December. 'Only things seem to have calmed down a bit now. No more disasters for a while.'

Fliss nodded.

'I really think we should. As long as we can get things moving. It's already a bit late, I s'pose. Maybe do some bargain weekends or Christmas breaks. What do you think? An all-in deal for say, four days? Parties, celebration meals, a murder mystery evening, maybe?' she suggested.

'How can we do all that and advertise in so short a space of time?' Sally gasped.

'Send brochures out to all our old

customers. Use the Internet, advertise locally. Loads of people leave everything to the last minute. Come on, Mum, this is it, make or break. If there's any chance it might be our last one here. Let's make it a Christmas to remember.'

'I hope you don't mean that it could be our last one here.'

Sally frowned and then cheered up.

'OK, you're on. Better get a brochure put together quickly, and food. I'd better plan menus and get the orders in. This is just so typical of you, spilling out all your ideas at the last minute. What about our present guests? Do you think we can ask them to leave at short notice, or do we let them stay on at the reduced rates?'

'Certainly not that. If they want to stay, they'll have to pay the full price. My guess is, we won't see them for dust.'

'I hope you're right,' Sally said.

The next couple of days were a mad frenzy of organisation. The whole thing had come together incredibly well. Fliss had spent every lunch hour she was at work, rushing to the shops, buying extras or making long lists of things to do. Sally, being the more tactful of the partnership, had agreed to give the news to the two ladies and to Matt.

Fliss had continued to work hard to forget her attraction to Matt and was avoiding him as much as possible, although she still felt that same jolt of excitement when she met him unexpectedly. She really did try hard to ignore it but it was not easy. She worked at saying nothing controversial and confined any conversation to asking if his work was going well. He was rather withdrawn, totally wrapped up in his plot and his computer was often heard clattering, late into the night.

'Bad news, I'm afraid,' Sally told Fliss one evening. 'Wyn and Elaine are refusing to budge. What's more, they fully expect to pay the same reduced rate over the whole Christmas period.

They say it's their right as long-established guests.'

'But that's ridiculous. They are each in a double room. They can't expect to stay at the same price for all that time. They're not sitting tenants, even if they might think they are. Besides, it means we'd only have four more double rooms to let out. We simply can't afford it, not with all the extras we're laying on. I'll go and tell them what I think of their attitude.'

'No, don't, Fliss. You are not the most tactful soul at the best of times. We'll sort something out.'

'But how can we risk letting the rooms to anyone else, if they refuse to move?'

'We can't. They'll just have to accept that they must pay the full, going rate for the festivities. I shall insist. Matt was absolutely fine about it. He wants to stay on and is happy to pay the extra rates. He also wants Jason to stay and says they can always share the room if we do manage to let the rest. He thinks it's a jolly sort of Christmas compared with his usual one.'

'Good,' Fliss said, finding a lump in her throat quite unexpectedly.

Perhaps, with all the celebrations, he might come round a bit. A warm Christmas with all the traditions might mellow him a little. Maybe he would have finished his book, too. That might make him less tense.

Just over a week before Christmas, the available rooms were all fully booked. There were even two extra couples on the reserve list, waiting to see if the two ladies would decide to leave.

'I simply can't force them to go,' Sally said in despair to Matt one morning.

'They are a strange pair, I must say. I don't understand why they want to stay on. They don't strike me as the party types. In fact they don't seem very happy about anything at all. I'll see if I can pump them a bit. They seem to like me, for some reason.'

'It's your masculine charm, dear,' Sally told him.

As he left her, she watched him go. Her mind drifted to the fantasy she'd once had — Matt and Fliss married and settled here, all running the hotel together. Now, unless Christmas really did work for them, it was unlikely any of them would be able to stay at the hotel.

To everyone's surprise, a couple of days later, the two ladies arrived in reception with a pile of luggage.

'We've really had enough of this dismal hole,' Wyn began. 'Shocking service, poor conditions. One long string of problems and inconveniences and now, after our loyalty, we're virtually being thrown out.'

'I beg your pardon?' Sally stuttered. 'Your loyalty? We've really done all we can to make you comfortable. You know perfectly well that there have been a series of unavoidable problems.'

'Rank amateurs,' Elaine chimed in. 'You'd never make it into any good hotel guides, not if you were the last hotel in Cornwall. We're also complaining to the agency who gave us your name,' she added in triumph. 'We want you removed from their list.'

'I'm sorry you feel that way. I assume you're planning to settle your bill now? I'll just print it out for you. Only take a moment,' Sally said calmly.

'Less a twenty per cent discount at the very least,' Wyn suggested.

'I'm sorry, I couldn't possibly manage that sort of discount,' Sally stammered. 'You're on the very lowest rate we offer. We're barely making money as it is.'

'Not a penny more than eighty per cent of our bill will be paid,' Elaine announced. 'I've been feeling sick with the cold for weeks now. I expect pneumonia to strike at any moment. And you should try to vary your menu, if you want to continue. People get sick of the same old fish every day.'

Sally's jaw dropped. She never served fish more than twice a week, as the main dish, and she'd always offered to cook something different if the choice for the evening meal was unpopular.

'What's going on?' Fliss asked, as she came into reception.

'Miss Derricoat and Miss Slater are leaving us. They're dissatisfied with the service.'

'Huh!' Fliss exploded. 'But that's great. It means we can let the rooms after all.'

The two women glared at her. Sally also gave her a look which firmly suggested that she disappear for a few minutes. She slipped behind the door and continued to listen to the argument. In the end, Sally agreed to knock off the last two days' fees as being only part of a week. Swiftly they looked at each other, as if realising this was the most they'd get. They both nodded and passed over a credit card.

Both kept looking at their watches and hurrying Sally on. It seemed odd after their initial desire to spend time negotiating their bill. Then there had been a total lack of haste. But now, getting out speedily seemed important, as if something was bothering them. Fliss ran upstairs, struck by the thought that they could have taken some of the hotel property. Bath towels were a favourite but there were plenty of other easily-lifted things.

Then, on the landing outside their rooms, Fliss could smell smoke. She hit the fire alarm and rushed to open the ladies' doors. They seemed to be jammed. This was the last thing they needed. The whole place could go up in flames. The old timbers in the building were very vulnerable. She grabbed the fire extinguisher and hurled herself against the door, just as Matt came out of his room.

'What on earth's going on?' he demanded.

'Dunno. Fire of some sort, and the two ladies are making a hasty getaway, and it's in their room.'

Matt added his weight to the door and it crashed inwards. Somehow, Wyn had managed to wedge the door before she had left it. The room was full of smoke and Fliss began to choke. She looked desperately round for the source of the smoke. The waste bin seemed to provide the answer. Wildly, she squirted the extinguisher at the basket, covering practically the entire area with foam.

Slowly the smoke died down and they could see the mess made by the dirty smoke. The room would need redecorating and much of the bedding had also suffered from being scorched by the initial fire.

'She stuffed some fabric into the basket, to stop the flames from burning out too quickly, I s'pose. Looks like a towel. Everything quite ruined, of course.'

Matt stared helplessly at the ruins of the pretty room.

'Damn the woman,' Fliss fumed. 'And to think I was wondering if she had merely stolen a few towels. They suddenly seemed in such a hurry to leave at the end. I was suspicious.'

She began a burst of coughing.

'Hadn't we better try to stop them?'

Matt spluttered, also catching the smoke at the back of his throat.

'Oh, crumbs, thanks. 'Course I should.'

Eyes streaming and still coughing like mad, Fliss staggered along the corridor to the stairs.

'Hang on. Shouldn't we check the other room for damage? Elaine may have laid some sort of booby trap as well.'

Fliss stopped and pulled out her keys. She unlocked the door and tried to push it open without success.

'Out of the way,' Matt ordered and hurled himself against the old wooden door.

There was no smoke this time. In fact, everything looked in order but then came the sound of running water.

'The bathroom,' Fliss squeaked.

She rushed over and soon found she was splashing through water. She pushed open the bathroom door. The bath was overflowing, as was the sink, the taps fully on. Bedding was stuffed

163

into every corner of the room so that the water had soaked into everything slowly, causing maximum damage to the carpets. She waded through the water and reached the taps.

'I don't believe this. What sort of people are they?'

But Matt had gone. He had rushed downstairs to try and catch the two women before they could make their getaway.

'Whatever's going on?' Sally asked, meeting him halfway down the stairs. 'What's all the banging around? And can I smell smoke?'

'Where are those two women?' he asked.

'Gone. They paid their bill and left. Why?'

'One of them tried to burn the place down, the other tried flooding it.'

He rudely elbowed past her and ran out of the door. He gazed down the lane but they had disappeared.

'Did you see them?' Sally asked running after him.

' 'Fraid not. They made a clean getaway. Must have had the car packed before they informed you they were leaving. We should get back to Fliss. She was trying to drown herself once she'd filled her lungs with smoke.'

'Heavens!' Sally called out. 'Is she all right?'

They went quickly back inside and rushed up the stairs. Fliss was still coughing fit to burst and had managed to pull the plugs out to let the water drain out of bath and basin.

'Oh, Mum, I'm so sorry,' she wailed, almost in tears. 'What are we going to do now?'

'Call the police for a start,' Matt said firmly.

'What good would that do?' Fliss asked.

'They won't get away with it. They've been very strange from the start. My guess is that they are responsible for all the damage that has been caused over the past weeks. Fridges, freezers, the untimely arrival of the health inspector, you name it, they could have caused the lot.'

'I suppose so. I'll go and phone them right away. Then we'd better get cleaning up.'

The police were helpful though not very hopeful of catching the two women.

'I wouldn't be surprised if they gave false names, to cover their tracks. I don't suppose you have their car number, do you?'

'Actually, I do remember it,' Matt said, surprising both Sally and Fliss. 'I have a bit of a thing for car numbers.'

He gave it to the policeman who immediately made a call to get the number checked. A few moments later, he had the answer.

'It's registered to someone in Redruth.'

'But that's only a few miles away. I don't understand. Why would those two be staying here if they lived locally? It's cost them a lot of money.'

Fliss frowned.

'I suppose it won't take you long to find them, in that case.'

'Unfortunately, it isn't that simple,' the officer replied. 'The owner of the vehicle evidently lives in a house that was demolished about five years ago. There's definitely a case of fraud, malicious damage, and probably anything you care to name. We shall do our best to catch them as soon as possible. I don't understand why you didn't report these various events earlier.'

'They thought it was my fault,' Sally explained. 'They thought I was going potty, I expect.'

'We didn't, Mum. Don't be silly.'

Fliss was looking guilty. She had thought exactly that but now felt thoroughly ashamed.

'Well,' the officer said, 'I suggest you get on to your insurance people and start sorting out the damage. Bad time of year for you, I expect. Bit close to Christmas to have to start spring cleaning.'

'We'll probably have to cancel Christmas,' Sally said with a groan. 'There's so much to do anyhow, without all this extra mess to clear up.'

9

We're not cancelling anything,' Fliss
said firmly. 'I'm going to get someone
in to sort it out everything. The
insurance will just have to fork out. I
take it we do have proper insurance
now?'

'I think so, dear.'

After all the nightmares, three days
later, the hotel was looking almost back
to its usual self. The insurance company
was finally persuaded to pay for
cleaners and decorators to do the
emergency work. The bed linen that
could be salvaged was laundered and
replacement carpeting organised. In the
meantime, Sally went back to her
menu-planning and prepared as much
as she could.

Fliss worked hard at the radio station
and did several more broadcasts. To her
delight, she was offered the permanent

job, which she had no hesitation in accepting. If they needed extra help in the hotel, she would be happy to organise it, knowing she was now able to earn a reasonable salary.

'I just hope everything is going to be all right for Christmas,' Sally said distractedly. 'Oh, no, I didn't order extra crackers for the extra guests.'

'It's going to be brilliant, Mum,' Fliss insisted. 'I finish work the day before Christmas Eve so I'll be able to help you with all the last-minute stuff and anything that's been overlooked.'

'And Jason and I will also lend a hand,' Matt said, coming into the room from behind them. 'It'll be fun to put up decorations and do all the Christmas stuff we have missed out on for years. Now, have you got any champagne in your cellar?'

' 'Course we have,' Sally said with a grin.

'Then get a bottle up here and we'll have a little celebration. I posted off my manuscript yesterday.'

She went off to the cellar.

'Well done,' Fliss said sincerely, 'in spite of the dramas that affect your life in this so-called tranquil place.'

'Maybe it actually helps,' he suggested.

'Are you going to tell me your pseudonym now?'

'No,' Matt said firmly.

'Why not? Are you ashamed of it?'

He stared at her. He was obviously fighting with his conscience.

'Well, it's Mae Morris. I'm Mae Morris,' he said suddenly.

'What?' She gasped. 'How can you be? I mean, she's so very feminine. I've always thought so.'

'Now you know why I keep quiet about it. Do you think women would read my stuff if they knew I was a man?'

'I dunno. It's still the same book, whoever wrote it, though it feels strange to think of you writing all those female-oriented novels, and the latest one, right here, under our roof.'

'Does it make any difference to how

you feel about me?' he asked.

She stared into his gorgeous eyes and gave a small smile.

'None at all. However futile it may seem at this moment, I'm so sorry I made so many stupid mistakes before. You must despise me thoroughly, for being such a leaper to wrong conclusions.'

'I don't despise you at all, in fact, just the opposite. Looking back, there is a degree of humour to the situation. I do regret the time we've wasted, however.'

'What do you mean?'

'Despite everything, I think I'm falling in love with you, Fliss. I hope I'm not too old and past it for you to love me back, just a little bit?'

He pulled her towards him and very gently pressed his lips against hers. Her whole body seemed to float high above herself and she imagined she could see herself wrapped in the arms of this man she loved so dearly. Was she dreaming, imagining this was happening? After all her stupid assumptions and accusations, she surely could never hope to really have this man so close. She opened her eyes and spoke breathlessly.

'I fell in love with you weeks ago,' she confessed. 'And of course you're not old and past it. You're only a few years older than me. Besides, it means you'll reach your pension all the sooner.'

They kissed again, laughing as they drew close.

'You do know I had to fight every scrap of conscience to resist you?' she told him.

'Oh, yes? I haven't entirely forgiven you for thinking so badly of me. There were two issues, I seem to remember. That I, a presumed married man, could take you out and even want to kiss you, and you even suspected I could be capable of damaging your property, if I remember rightly.'

'I'm sorry. I was so stupid. Unforgivable?' she said with a question in her voice. 'I think I wanted to kiss you more than anything.'

He reached over to her and drew her close. His lips felt warm against hers and his body strong and firm.

Sally came into the room and stared.

'Don't tell me you two have finally come to your senses. Took you long enough, I must say.'

'What on earth do you mean?' Fliss demanded.

'Well, all that skirting round each other. I began to wonder if you were quite normal, Fliss. I mean to say, it was obvious you were meant for each other after the first couple of days.'

'Sit down, both of you. I have something to say.'

Matt's tone brooked no argument and they sat down on the stools. He took the bottle of champagne from Sally and went behind the bar to find three glasses. He popped the cork open, filled the flutes and handed them round.

'To another successful Mae Morris story,' Fliss said raising her glass.

'I thought she was the author you especially liked,' Sally said, looking puzzled.

'Oh, he is,' she agreed.

'He?'

'Matt is none other than Mae Morris. No wonder she always refused to be interviewed.'

'When I can get a word in, there's something I'd like to say, to you both. Felice, Sally, please listen. Will you marry me, Fliss? And will you be my mother-in-law, Sally?'

Mother and daughter looked at each other and laughed out loud.

'What's the deal if one of us says no?' Fliss asked.

'I stay on at the hotel and annoy you, until one of you gives in.'

'I'll have you as a son-in-law, soon as you like,' Sally said firmly.

'Doesn't look as if I have a choice then, does it?' Fliss teased.

Matt flung his arms round her and held her close.

'Oh, Fliss, thank you. You've made me very happy. And you, too, Sally. Now, if you'll allow me, I'd like to invest in the hotel and, please, may we all live here together? With some money to spend on it, we can do a lot of modernisation and get in some extra help. What do you say?'

'It's exactly what I had planned when you first came to stay,' Sally told them. 'I realised that this was going to be the perfect solution to all our problems. I knew it was a case of waiting for you to come to your senses. That's the trouble with young people today. Never can make up their minds.'

Fliss stared at her mother. She would never quite get accustomed to the surprises.

'But Matt's only been here for a few weeks, even if it does seem like for ever. Actually, all the things that have happened since you arrived add up to more than usually goes on here in months.'

'Must be the writer's vibes.'

He was interrupted by the ringing of the telephone. Sally went to answer it. Her reaction to the call made both Matt and Fliss go to her side.

'What is it, Mum?'

'The police have caught the two women. I'll tell you later. Sorry, officer. Do go on.'

His voice went on for a few minutes then Sally exclaimed.

'Good heavens. But they were always such a friendly lot. Really? Good gracious. Who'd have believed it?'

The one-sided conversation nearly drove Fliss mad. She kept tugging at her mother's arm. At last Sally finished and put down the phone. To their irritation, she went back to the bar and picked up the bottle.

'For pity's sake, Mother, what's going on?'

'Wyn and Elaine, whatever their real names are, have been caught. It seems they are closely related to the people who keep that pub and bed-and-breakfast place in the next village. They hoped to buy this place at a knock-down price. When they heard we were struggling and offering cut-price deals for the winter, they thought it was the ideal opportunity of doing what they could to discredit us. They hoped to buy the place, modernise it and open it as some sort of beach bar. Our plans for Christmas looked like being a success and they saw that as the final straw. Hence their dramatic departure. We'd certainly have dented their own seasonal trade, I expect. The final acts of sabotage were desperation rearing its head.'

'So, do we get any sort of compensation?' Fliss asked.

'There'll be a court case, naturally. I s'pose it will be up to the insurance company to make their claims. We shall have to try to recover the cost of their bill, too. The credit card they used was inevitably a stolen one.'

'But you must have put it through the scanner.'

'Of course, but it hadn't been reported till this morning.'

'But what about the name on it?' Fliss demanded.

'I was so flustered, I s'pose I didn't

check it properly.'

'Oh, Mum,' her daughter chided. 'Really.'

'Poor, silly women,' Sally said.

'You are a remarkable lady,' Matt told her. 'All that aggravation and you can still feel sympathy.'

'Well, they were probably desperate, unfulfilled, I don't know.'

'I love you, Mum,' Fliss said, surprising herself. 'I don't think I've actually said that lately, have I? Not out loud.'

'No. I don't suppose either of us says it too often but is it really necessary? I mean we both know, don't we?'

'Your daughter is so good at jumping to the wrong conclusion, I should make sure you say it quite often. I certainly intend to.'

'Am I being presumptuous in thinking we are now engaged?' Fliss asked. 'Or is that another conclusion I shouldn't have leaped to?'

'I suppose we are. Why?'

'I was thinking that it might be rather a coup to interview my fiancé on live radio. I mean, very few women can have married one of the country's leading romantic fiction writers.'

'But my cover would be blown apart. I may never sell another book.'

'They say sales always pick up when a writer disappears mysteriously. You could then return as someone else — Matt Morris, Mae's long-lost brother, devastated by her loss, for instance.'

'Tell me, Fliss, have you ever thought of writing fiction yourself? You'd probably beat me hollow. But, yes, OK. I'll blow my cover, just for you. It's time I came into the open. After ten novels, I guess my reputation is pretty solid.'

'I hope I might get them to give me a regular spot on the radio. I was thinking that I could base part of it on the people we have staying here. When we're really successful, we should get our share of celebrities who want somewhere peaceful to stay. If I promised not to put the tapes out until after they'd left, I don't see they could object. And ordinary people are pretty interesting, too. I mean to say, who'd have thought that the very boring Wyn Slater and Elaine Derricoat could have been such crooks?'

'Sounds like a winner to me,' Matt agreed. 'So, I'm to be your first so-called coup, am I?'

* * *

Sally was up well before dawn on Christmas morning. She put turkeys into the oven; prepared vegetables by the hundredweight and put on several home-made puddings to steam. She felt happier than she had felt in many months, even years. When Fliss came down to find her, she was humming carols as she worked.

'Can you come up to the sitting room for a few minutes?' Fliss asked. 'We thought it would be nice to swop presents before breakfast started occupying everyone.'

'I'm doing a very easy breakfast. Bucks Fizz, strawberries and croissants all round. Nothing to prepare, as it's all ready to go. Shall I bring ours up with me?'

In the small sitting room they used in their apartment, Matt and Jason were waiting. Matt had bought a tiny tree, decorated with fairy lights which added the perfect festive touch. A heap of brightly-wrapped presents filled the table by the side of the tree. They all drank Bucks Fizz and exchanged presents with a great deal of happy laughter. Matt suddenly left the room and came back to hand Fliss a large box, wrapped in Christmas paper. It all seemed to be moving rather strangely.

'What on earth?' she murmured as a loud miaow came from the box.

'You'll have to open it quickly,' Jason told her. 'We barely managed to wrap it before you came in and they were determined to make a break for freedom, immediately.'

Fliss pulled the top off and the two kittens, now considerably larger, stepped out into the bright light. They immediately pounced on the parcels and began to tear them, leaping in the air and falling back.

'How on earth did you manage this?' Fliss asked in surprise.

'I phoned the RSPCA last week and asked if they still had them. You seemed so disappointed when they had to go.'

'I love them. Thank you, Matt. Hope you don't mind, Mum?'

' 'Course not. Matt asked me first. He's a very thoughtful man.'

'And there's this, as well,' Matt said, unusually shy, as he handed her a small package.

'Oh, it's beautiful,' Fliss gasped, slipping the unwrapped engagement ring on to her finger. 'I adore sapphires.'

'Your mum told me that, too.'

'Is there anything about me that she didn't tell you?' Fliss asked, pretending to be cross

'What you'd want to call the kittens. I suggested Holly and Ivy but she thought you'd say that was too twee.'

'The only possible names are Wyn and Elaine, don't you think? After all, if it hadn't been for them, probably none of this would have happened.'

Fliss smiled and took Matt's hand.

'I'm so glad you wanted to come and stay awhile.'

'Oh, goodness, I must get to the kitchen or the turkeys will never be cooked. Everyone will be wanting breakfast, too,' Sally exclaimed.

'We'll all help,' Matt offered. 'Full room service.'

'I think this is going to be the best Christmas ever,' Fliss said happily.

'If those wretched turkeys ever get cooked in time!' the others echoed.

THE END

We do hope that you have enjoyed reading this large print book.

Did you know that all of our titles are available for purchase?

We publish a wide range of high quality large print books including:
Romances, Mysteries, Classics
General Fiction
Non Fiction and Westerns

Special interest titles available in large print are:
The Little Oxford Dictionary
Music Book, Song Book
Hymn Book, Service Book

Also available from us courtesy of Oxford University Press:
Young Readers' Dictionary
(large print edition)
Young Readers' Thesaurus
(large print edition)

For further information or a free brochure, please contact us at:
Ulverscroft Large Print Books Ltd.,
The Green, Bradgate Road, Anstey,
Leicester, LE7 7FU, England.
Tel: (00 44) 0116 236 4325
Fax: (00 44) 0116 234 0205

Other titles in the
Linford Romance Library:

VISIONS OF THE HEART

Christine Briscomb

When property developer Connor Grant contracted Natalie Jensen to landscape the grounds of his large country house near Ashley in South Australia, she was ecstatic. But then she discovered he was acquiring — and ripping apart — great swathes of the town. Her own mother's house and the hall where the drama group met were two of his targets. Natalie was desperate to stop Connor's plans — but she also had to fight the powerful attraction flowing between them.

FINGALA, MAID OF RATHAY

Mary Cummins

On his deathbed, Sir James Montgomery of Rathay asks his daughter, Fingala, to swear that she will not honour her marriage contract until her brother Patrick, the new heir, returns from serving the King. Patrick must marry. Rathay must not be left without a mistress. But Patrick has fallen in love with the Lady Catherine Gordon whom the King, James IV, has given in marriage to the young man who claims to be Richard of York, one of the princes in the Tower.